Red

A Fractured Fairy Tale

J.E. Taylor

JET-FUELED FICTION

Red

What happens when a werewolf hunter falls for her prey?

Red Locklear regularly hunts all manner of woodland prey, but her favorite kill is the beast that tore her parents apart when she was a little girl.

The werewolf.

Now that Red is all grown up, these horrid creatures are terrorizing Dakota Territory once again. As a member of the elite Dakota Guard, Red has a duty to extinguish the life of every last wolf she sees. Failing to do so is a death sentence.

When her grandmother doesn't come back from a foraging run, Red dons her quiver of silver arrows and breaks town law, heading into the forest after sunset to search for her.

The dark woods test her hunting skills as well as her loyalty to the Dakota Guard, and she's left wondering if there is any way out of this alive.

Chapter 1

"WE HAVEN'T HEARD FROM her in months," Pa said, unaware I was just outside my parents' bedroom door.

"You have told me a thousand times how dangerous those mountain passes can be," my mother said in her exasperated voice. "What if we get caught in a storm?"

"The almanac said we have at least another six weeks before the winter rolls in. So now is the perfect time to visit. Besides, my mother hasn't even met Ruby yet. Don't you think it's time?"

A sigh followed.

I coughed, covering my mouth a second too late, and silence settled on the bedroom. The creak of springs sounded, and the soft swish of fabric against the floorboards crossed closer to the door. I darted my eyes around the darkened hallway for a place to hide, my nightmare that brought me to their room forgotten in my panic of being caught listening to their private conversation.

My father opened the door before I could escape into the shadows. "Ruby, what are you doing out of bed?"

"I had a nightmare," I whispered and studied the shadows in the wood grain on the floor.

"You need as much rest as you can get before we head to your grandmother's house in the morning. We need you sharp on this trip. Otherwise, we might not be eating for the next few days," he said.

I narrowed my eyes at him and glanced at my mother on the bed. The dim lantern illuminated her face and made her deep auburn hair blend into the wood frame of their bed.

"I can hit a squirrel at fifty yards while sleep walking," I said when I brought my gaze back to Pa. Sleep had nothing to do with the quality of my hunting skills.

Pa put his hand on my back with a chuckle and led me back to my bedroom. "I still want you to rest. Dakota is a long ride, and if you are too tired to aim straight, we will be a very hungry family when we get to your grandmother's house."

"Pa?" I asked as he tucked me tightly under the covers. "My teacher, Mrs. Kettle, said there are monsters in the woods surrounding Dakota."

His smile faded and he blinked like he had an eyelash in his eye. "Why would your teacher tell you that?"

I shrugged. "We were studying the territories bordering Weber, and she explained the trails to get to the towns in each territory. She went clockwise starting with Alberta to the northeast and ended with Dakota to the northwest. She said the road to Dakota is swallowed by a forest full of monsters."

He let out another chuckle, but this time it wasn't amused. "It's bear country, sweetie."

He leaned over and gave me a kiss on the cheek, leaving me without a real answer. Weber was bear country, too. No one said Weber was full of monsters. The teacher had said the road wound over the mountains and through a river before it disappeared into woods as dark as night. I remember the flash in her eyes and the whisper she likely hadn't intended for anyone to hear.

I didn't think she was talking about bears. My heart clanged at the thought of traveling through a monster-filled forest.

I tried to push the thoughts away and rest like my father asked, but the images that kept running past my eyelids were worse than the original nightmare that had woken me.

I RODE IN FRONT of my mother on the edge of Bessy's saddle. While the old mare made for a smooth ride, I still ended the day stiff from the journey. My brother, Roy, got the better end of the deal. He got to ride with Pa on Midnight, the fastest steed in all of Weber territory.

Pa never let me ride that horse. He always said I wasn't old enough or big enough to stay on his back, especially when he went into a full gallop.

Figures. My brother had all the luck. At least he didn't have my skills with a bow and arrow. I could shoot rings around him and proved it with a plump rabbit for dinner on the first night and three squirrels the second night.

The third night, we slept in sight of the Dakota border where the road faded into the trees. I was thankful we stopped outside of those woods. On the plateau where we camped, wild life was scarce, so all we ended up with for dinner was a rattlesnake that Pa killed earlier in the day.

The fire crackled, and my gaze kept drifting to the forest in the distance. Neither the height of the mountains nor the icy chill of the river we had crossed brought forth the same level of trepidation as that dense wall of trees. I shivered, wrapping my arms tighter around my chest. I snuggled into the blankets and turned to face the fire, dismissing the thought of monsters.

"CAN I RIDE MIDNIGHT today?" I asked.

"I don't think so, Ruby."

My stomach clenched and so did my teeth. My father attached the travel sack to Midnight's saddle and glanced at me. He must have seen my aggravation because he offered me the same old story.

"You're not big enough to handle Midnight, sweetheart."

"Roy got to ride him when he was eight," I said.

"Roy was bigger than you are at eight. Go help your mother pack the rest of our things."

I stomped away loud enough to make my dissatisfaction known, but not enough to get a swat on my butt for my behavior. I didn't talk, even as we approached the thick forest. The path seemed to disappear, and I shivered.

"We only have two more days before we can bask in the warmth of your grandmother's fireplace," Pa said and locked his gaze with mine before he coaxed Midnight into the lead.

Roy turned and gave me a smile, like going into monster-filled woods was a cool thing. I knew with a cold certainty that I wasn't getting a lick of sleep tonight.

Every branch snap jerked my form, and I struggled to see what was beyond the narrow channel. I constantly scanned the deep green brush like I was hunting for small game, but in reality, I was searching for creatures with a more violent nature.

When we finally trotted into a small clearing and dismounted, Roy took the horses and tied them to the nearest branch. My father handed me the bow and arrow. With the weapon in my hand, all the deep fear tightening my muscles gave way to a calmness I welcomed. I crept around the perimeter of our little circle while my parents started to set up camp.

I caught movement on my right. Before my brain registered the animal, my arrow had pinned the rabbit to the earth. A clean head shot. I grinned, picking it up and bringing it back to the family with a real sense of accomplishment.

Clouds rolled in before the last light bled from the sky, and the full moon seemed to play hide-and-seek in the foggy cover. We ate in silence, savoring the tender meat and licking the juices from our fingers.

With full bellies, we settled into our makeshift beds and gave in to the exhaustion. I stared at what I could see of the man on the moon until my eyes could no longer stay open.

The horses whinnying pulled me from sleep. I darted my gaze at the shadows made by the fire, and I shivered in the cold night air despite the heavy blanket draped over me. The hairs on my arms prickled as the horses grew more restless. Something had them spooked.

I patted my father's leg. "Pa," I whispered on the still air. My heart picked up the pace.

"Get some more sleep, Ruby," he muttered.

"Something is spooking the horses."

My father rolled over and glanced at me and then the horses beyond me. A crease appeared between his eyes, but he gave me a reassuring smile before he gently shook my mother awake.

"I think we've had enough rest," he whispered.

My mother looked at him, blinked, and then her eyes widened. It was as if a lightning bolt shot out of the sky and catapulted her to her feet. The instant she was standing, she started gathering our things as if the woods were burning down around us.

"Roy, go get the horses." My father swatted my brother's back. "Ruby, you go stay by your mother."

My brother got to his unsteady feet. He yawned and shuffled to the tree where we had Midnight and Bessy tied up.

I stepped towards my mother, close enough to the dying fire to feel the heat radiating from the coals. Her arms wrapped around me tighter than usual while my brother pulled the horses closer. Their hoofs stomped the ground in nervous beats.

My father hoisted me onto the back of Midnight and my heart jumped into my throat. Alarms sounded in my head when Pa told Roy to hop on Midnight with me. Roy handed Bessy's reins to my mother and stepped towards where Pa held onto Midnight's bridle.

Roy only made it halfway across the clearing when the monsters attacked. A clawed paw severed my brother's throat. A plume of blood shot from the wound, dousing the fire. He didn't have time to scream. I would never forget my mother's cry. The pitch started as one of loss, but soon morphed to a sharp pain-filled wail.

My father smacked Midnight's flank just before a wall of grey fur took him down. The stallion flew forward. I grabbed for the horse's mane to catch my balance.

Midnight's speed was no match for the massive wolves that pursued me. Their radiant blue eyes pierced the darkness as the gap widened until I couldn't hear their snarls over the throbbing beat of my heart in my own ears. My harsh sobs filled the woods along with the steady pounding of Midnight's hoofs. He didn't slow until we arrived at Dakota's darkened town center.

Monsters did exist, and I would never forget their murderous eyes or their equally heinous growls.

Chapter 2

"I AM PERFECTLY CAPABLE of going foraging on my own. Besides, aren't you supposed to be going on that hunting trip with the rest of the archers?" Grandmother asked me as she tidied up the breakfast nook. She turned, her silver corkscrew curls falling over her shoulders, and leveled her grey-eyed stare in my direction. One silver eyebrow rose.

My grandmother was the epitome of strength and grace, even though she was nearing her eighties. The woman was feisty and brave, everything I hoped I would be if I was blessed enough to reach her age.

I shifted my stance and crossed to the table with the breakfast plates. “I know you’re capable, Gram. But it’s really not safe out there. Not with the werewolves terrorizing Dakota.”

“Pft.” She waved me off and took the seat across from me.

“I’m serious. We lost Mickey last week, and those bastards are getting bolder by the minute.”

She waggled her finger at me. “Watch your language, girl.” She dug into the eggs in the center serving bowl.

I sighed and studied Gram’s coveted curls. I envied her hair. Mine fell straight as one of the arrows in my quiver, and the color was the cause of my nickname.

Red.

And not the beautiful auburn red my mother had had. No, it was more akin to a forest fire. I had a hell of a time blending in the forest for most seasons, but now that fall was upon us, my hair resembled the burnt orange of the leaves.

"You really should go with someone else, Gram," I said and focused on the food instead of her perfect hair.

"They need you on the hunt. You know you are more skilled than anyone else in this town," she said and took a bite of her breakfast.

Gram had no idea how deep on the side of trouble I was with the Dakota Guard. If I missed another hunt, the head of the Guard, Remy Steele, warned that I would have to turn in my archer's bow. It was the one thing I was good at, and losing that would be like losing my family all over again.

But with the audacity of this particular pack, the idea of having my grandmother out in the berry patch alone didn't settle well. If I stayed and protected her instead of doing my job, I would lose the only status I had in this town. If I let her go alone, I could lose the only family I had left.

My chest tightened, and I sent her a strained smile, waving her off with a sheepish nod. I had a job to do, and the town was counting on me.

Dakota didn't have any outside help. We were too secluded in the deep northwestern forest. Mountains blocked us to the east, and ravines blocked us to the west. The nearest settlement was a good three-day ride at a full gallop through treacherous mountain terrain.

And Dakota was under siege for the first time since my parents died.

Sure, we had had rogue werewolves in the area over the years, but since that horrible night when I was eight, there hadn't been a pack in the vicinity.

Until now. And they were a nasty bunch.

With the fading of the summer heat, people started disappearing. The ones we found were mauled beyond what the local bears usually did. It wasn't until we heard the howls in the distance that we knew what was killing the town's people.

Thirteen years of training had led me to this moment, and my grandmother wasn't going to let me babysit her when I could be out there taking down the monsters. One glance from her told me I was right.

"You need to go." She didn't leave me any choice.

"Fine," I mumbled despite the discomfort scraping my skin. I ignored the warning bells and dug into my food.

We ate the rest of the meal in silence, each of us lost in our own thoughts. Mine tumbled between what I had to do today and the fall harvest. I wasn't sure if Travis was going to ask me to the town dance or not. I secretly hoped he would move on. While he was the closest friend I had, there just were no sparks in it for me. He, on the other hand, had hinted endlessly to me about a future. I wasn't ready to settle down. At least not with anyone from Dakota.

Gram cleared her throat. "You were about a million miles away, weren't you?"

Heat filled my cheeks, and I let out a laugh. "Yes, sorry."

"Thinking about your parents?" she asked.

I flinched at the mention of my family. "No. Travis." I didn't expand any further, but my tone said it all.

Gram cocked her head like one of the neighborhood puppies. "What's wrong with Travis?"

"Nothing. He just isn't... you know..." I said and shrugged as I picked at the food on my plate.

"He has become such a sweet man," she said.

I rolled my eyes.

Gram was a fan of Travis's and had been for as long as I could remember. Too bad it didn't change the way I felt. I took another bite of breakfast.

Gram opened her mouth to ask me another question, and I raised my hand, stopping her.

"I don't want to talk about Travis, okay?"

Gram inhaled enough to expand her chest in that manner that announced her disappointment. "Okay," she whispered, and we both focused on the plates in front of us.

After we finished, I cleaned the dishes in the basin and dried and stored them back in the pantry before dumping the dishwater out the window.

I crossed to the chair and pulled on my vest, hoping it would be enough to keep me warm in the cool fall air. I hated hunting with my thick wool coat that hung on the rack in the corner. With my quiver over my shoulder, I headed for the door.

"Ruby?"

I glanced back at Gram.

"Be careful," she said and gave me a small smile of support. The worry lines at the corners of her eyes belied the smile.

"I always am. You be careful, too, Gram."

She patted the sheath on her belt with a nod and finished gathering her basket for foraging berries in the grove. As I walked away from our cabin, a lump formed in the back of my throat. The same lump that always accompanied me on my way to the Guard, as if this could be the last time we see each other.

I swiped at the mist in my eyes and continued down the path leading through the woods directly into the center of Dakota. I steadied the bow in my hand, lining an arrow in place, keeping vigilant for any breaking branch, leaf rustle, or wicked growl.

TALK OF MY PARENTS had me jumpy as I traversed the winding wooded path into Dakota. The cloudy sky obscured the morning sun, reminding me of the night I lost my family to the wolves.

I picked up my pace. While I knew I was running a little behind, I wasn't sure just how late I would be, and getting out of these woods as fast as I could was a priority at the moment.

The last time I was late, I got paired with the worst archer on the Guard, and the day had been an exercise in dodging his arrows instead of werewolves. Not that any of our daily hunts had been fruitful in flushing out the pack. They were well hidden, and it was frustrating.

Hunting at night was not allowed, even though that seemed to be the time the pack was most active. Just the thought of being out with darkness surrounding me made me shiver.

I tried to focus on the impending hunt, but memories of my family's dying screams kept interrupting my train of thought.

I shook the bloody visions from my head as I stepped out of the woods and onto the gravel road that led into the center of town. With the tree canopy behind me, I stowed the arrow back in my quiver. I kept scanning the area, but I didn't have the same urgency to be vigilant as I did under the tree cover.

The sense of ever-present danger the woods instilled in me kept me alive all these years, but once I was in the town center, that edge faded. Nothing messed with my mind as much as the woods.

"Boo!"

I yelped and spun in the direction of the voice, reaching for one of my arrows.

Travis McGee burst out laughing from his vantage point next to the town hall. He stepped from the shadows, and his blond hair swirled in the breeze. His dark eyes crinkled with amusement, and his smile dimpled his cheeks.

"Damn it, Travis!" I held the arrow against my bow and glared at him. "I should shoot you for giving me a heart attack!"

Travis strolled up next to me with that ridiculous grin still plastered on his face. "You wouldn't dare," he said in a deep timbre.

I supposed I could see why some of the local girls swooned when he went by, but he just annoyed me like only a best friend could.

Instead of agreeing, I smacked his arm with the shaft of the arrow. "You're such a jerk," I muttered as we rounded the bend into the open courtyard where the rest of the Guard stood.

"You're late," a harsh voice rang out over the quiet assembly.

I glanced to my left, right into the annoyed eyes of Remy Steele. His face was lined with ancient wrinkles and his lips formed an unhappy sneer. He was perhaps the meanest Guardsman I had ever met. Most of the Guard was afraid of him, but not me. I just thought he was an ass who liked to exude authority.

He sauntered over and glared down at me with sharp green eyes. "This is the third time this week," he growled.

I could have uttered a litany of excuses and groveled for his forgiveness like I had seen countless others do, but we both knew I was the best shot in the lot, so he'd just have to deal with my tardiness. I gave him an offhanded shrug and continued past him.

"One of these days I'm going to take you over my knee," he hissed.

I spun on him. Threats, whether empty or not, riled me up. "You want to take care in what you say, Remy."

His eyes narrowed, and then he looked away.

I took that as a sign of retreat on his part and returned my attention to the rest of the horde. I was the lone woman among men, but they knew my past. They knew the talent in my steady hands. They knew I had their backs. And they knew my need for vengeance ran deep in my veins.

They had my back out there, too. Even Remy, who was as close to the definition of my nemesis as anyone in this town. He and Gram had a falling out years before I came along and he has held it against me ever since I entered the Guard.

It was Gram's insistence that allowed me to train with the Guard. She saw my raw talent with a bow and arrow after she and I had gone hunting for food. Remy had always treated me as if I stepped in the middle of the boy's club.

However, in moments of danger, Remy had always chosen to protect other members of the Guard instead of letting any one of us fall prey to wolves. I lost count of the number of times he saved me from an attacking wolf. He could say the same for me, as well.

"Red, since you and Travis were late, you two will pair up with me today on the hunt," Remy announced.

The relief of the other guardsmen hung on the air. No one liked pairing with Remy. Not only was he less than desirable company, he was a slave driver. Travis groaned under his breath while Remy paired up the rest of the hunters in parties of three.

"I don't have to tell you what's at stake here," Remy said, his sharp gaze landing on me before it moved on. "We need to flush these bastards out, because the longer they remain alive and in our territory, the more of our people die. If you run into a single wolf, kill it. If you run across the pack..." He took a deep breath, meeting each and every eye. "Take as many of them out as you can."

It was what he didn't say that sent a shiver up my spine. Three men, even three armed men, were no match against a full pack. Taking them on was suicide.

Every one of us accepted the responsibility to keep the town safe. The possibility of death was part of being a Dakota Guard. We all nodded our understanding.

After everyone dispersed in their assigned direction, Remy turned to me. “Ready to get your ass whooped?” He didn’t wait for an answer. Instead, he stomped off into the woods.

Travis and I followed, and dread wrapped a tight fist around my heart.

Chapter 3

After half the day had passed, I reached into the pack Gram put together for me and stole a bite of one of her oatmeal cookies while I followed Remy. Travis had my back, and I handed him half of the cookie as we rounded a bend, shoveling the rest in my mouth before Remy could turn and catch me eating on the job. Remy didn't like us doing anything that would occupy our hands, even if it only took a second.

His tirades about what could happen in that split second weren't without merit, but we had been going flat out since this morning and hadn't encountered a thing. Hunger could cause just as much trouble with wavering attention as our hands being occupied for a moment, so I chanced his wrath in favor of shutting off the grumbling in my stomach.

I never remembered Remy being amicable. Not even that first day that Gram dragged me into town and made me give the Guard a demonstration. He didn't even show the slightest interest, but the rest of the trainees were in awe that I could slice an apple in half, especially since it was thrown in the air. I did it a half dozen times to prove it wasn't a fluke.

"I CAN'T HAVE A child in the Guard," Remy said to my grandmother.

Gram looked around at the cluster of boys that were my age, and she waved her hand at them. "You already have children in the Guard. You mean you can't have a girl in your Guard," she argued with her hands on her hips.

"May," he started, but Gram wouldn't have any of it.

"She can run faster than any of them. And she's a better shot than even you ever were!"

Remy's face reddened brighter than any of the apples in Gram's basket. He grabbed one and pitched it with all his might towards the woods.

I didn't think. I just reacted and when two neat, halved slices fell to the ground and my arrow embedded in the tree that would have blocked the apple's progress, both my Gram and Remy stared at the apple and then turned towards me.

I just smiled and shrugged my shoulders at their matching slack jaws.

Remy's lips pressed together, and he glanced back at the decimated apple before studying the ground.

"Well?" Gram asked.

"Fine, but she isn't getting any special treatment. If she can't keep up with the boys, she's out."

Gram nodded and left me in Remy's care.

REMY SLOWED NEAR THE northern cliffs that lead to the ravine and leveled that same hostile look from all those years ago at both Travis and I.

"Did you bring any of your grandmother's treats?" he asked in a gruff, out-of-breath tone.

I reached into my bag and pulled another cookie out, debating on whether I would just eat it in front of him or not. But I knew better than to aggravate him even more than my simple presence did. Instead, I offered it to him.

He gave me a smile of appreciation, which was rare, and slightly frightening to view. His grin looked more like a toothy grimace than anything resembling genuine happiness, and it never quite reached his eyes. The only time I ever saw glee in his eyes was when he was killing a werewolf.

“What about me?” Travis asked.

I pulled the last cookie out and split it in half, handing him the smaller half this time.

Remy chuckled. He thought he was special getting a whole cookie. He didn’t know I shared one already with Travis. Neither of us corrected his silent gloating, either.

“I don’t think there’s anything in this direction,” I said as I scanned the wooded area behind us. This would be the perfect place to launch an assault. We had nowhere to run, and jumping from the cliff was just as much of an automatic death sentence as facing a pack.

We had been stopped long enough to make the hairs on my neck prickle. I didn’t want to just stand around waiting for the beasts to corner us, but Remy didn’t seem to be in any rush. Pushing him would only make him linger longer.

"One of you needs to climb that tree and do a scan before we head back, and since Red was kind enough to give me a whole cookie, I think it's Travis's turn to do something useful."

I raised an eyebrow. It was the first time I wasn't given the grunt task. I'd have to remember that in the future. Remy had a soft spot for Gram's cookies, and if I saved a whole one for him instead of just offering up half, I might get the lighter duty.

Travis didn't grumble or say anything snide like I would have been tempted to do. He just gave a nod and jumped in the air, catching the nearest limb with the inside of his elbow. His feet dangled above the ground, and he hoisted himself onto the branch.

It creaked under his weight. I bit my lip and scanned the woods for any movement. A snap brought my gaze back to Travis. His outstretched hand missed the next tree limb, and he dropped the ten feet to the ground, landing on his outstretched arm. A sharp crack was immediately followed by his yelp of pain.

Both Remy and I bolted to where Travis lay on the ground holding his arm to his chest. His lips were pressed together, but his red and scrunched face broadcasted his pain more than a scream would have. His forearm was bent at an unnatural angle, and a red stain spread on his sleeve.

"Damn it, boy," Remy growled and raked a hand through his hair. He took a deep breath and closed his eyes for a moment before his gaze turned to mine. "Make yourself useful and grab a couple of arrows."

I glanced at the half dozen arrows strewn on the ground and gathered them up as Remy squatted next to Travis. My heart drummed in my chest. The beasts could smell blood for miles. If they got Travis's scent either in human or wolf form, we would have a hell of a fight on our hands.

The tear of fabric pulled my gaze back to them, and the view of Travis's bone sticking out of his forearm made me regret eating Gram's cookie. I turned away and busied myself with picking up the fallen arrows. Normally, I wasn't a squeamish person, but because it was Travis, empathy crashed through me like a wild storm, making my stomach clench.

Travis's guttural whine made me spin towards him again. Remy had already done whatever it took to get the bone back inside Travis's arm, but my friend's face had gone ashen as a result.

"Get over here with those arrows," Remy barked.

I stepped to his side, handing the arrows to him.

He glared up at me. “Splint his arm.” He ripped the sleeves off his own shirt. “One arrow on the inside, one along the side and one on the outside, please,” he directed as I fiddled with the arrows.

When I had the right formation, Remy tied one of the sleeves around Travis’s wrist and the other just shy of his elbow, making a solid splint. Travis’s arm still oozed blood from the bone hole, but some of the color had returned to his face.

Remy helped him to a sitting position and Travis winced, holding his injured arm to his chest.

“I don’t think I can run with my arm like this.”

“We can’t leave you out here,” I said and immediately disliked the higher pitch of my voice. I knew that sound—it was my verge-of-panic tone.

“Travis needs a sling to stabilize his arm,” Remy said, eyeing me like I had a sling up my sleeve. “Give me your shirt.”

I blinked at him before the words sank in. While I was wearing a vest, just the thought of undressing in front of Travis and Remy left me cold. Travis wasn't expecting the directive either. His jaw hung open from the order.

"Why *my* shirt?"

"Because mine doesn't have sleeves anymore," Remy snapped. "The sooner you hand it over, the sooner we can start back. It's going to take us longer, which means you and I have to be sharp."

I glanced at Travis and turned my back, dropping my bow and quiver on the ground. As much as I didn't like obeying his command, I understood the rationale. My hands shook as I unbuttoned my vest. I put it between my knees and went to work on the shirt buttons. With a deep breath, I stripped the shirt and reached my arm behind me. A moment later, it was yanked from my hand. The vest wasn't nearly as warm as the combination with the shirt, and I shivered as I finished buttoning the rough fabric over my torso.

By the time I turned around, Remy had Travis on his feet and my shirt formed into a manageable sling with the sleeves tied at the back of his neck.

"Thanks, Red," Travis said.

His gaze remained on the ground, and I couldn't tell if he was just embarrassed by his accident or whether me stripping my shirt pushed him beyond discomfort.

“Think you can do this?” I asked.

“That’s a stupid question,” Remy growled. “He has no choice. Make sure you watch our backs.” He took the lead, leaving me staring after them as they entered the forest.

I threaded an arrow into my bow and followed Remy and Travis into the canopy, gulping down the fear that threatened to close my throat.

In the deep thicket, sounds echoed in my ears. Sweat soaked my forehead despite the chill in the air, occasionally dripping in my eyes. Each time the sting nearly closed my eyes, but I just gritted my teeth and dealt with it until the sting passed because taking either of my hands off my bow and arrow was not an option. My back was slick as well, and my wool vest clung to me like a scratchy sack.

A branch cracked to my right and I spun, letting my arrow fly. It whistled through the air, catching nothing. Both Remy and Travis stared at me.

“What in tarnation?” Remy growled.

Travis didn’t say anything. He was bathed in sweat as much as I was, and circles had formed under his eyes.

“I heard something,” I mumbled and focused on where my arrow had disappeared. I knew how few silver arrows we had amongst the three of us, and my wasted shot embarrassed me more than stripping my shirt had.

Thankfully, neither of them commented further. Instead, they turned back towards town and continued our slow jog. Remy swept his bow in an arc in front of him as he went. I followed, turning so my back faced both of them and mimicked Remy's sweep of the terrain.

Chapter 4

BY THE TIME WE entered the town square, the sun touched the horizon and my muscles were stiff from the intense vigilance. However, my discomfort wasn't even on the same plane as Travis's. His pasty features were marred by random blotches of red, and the dark circles under his eyes aged him by ten years or more.

“We need to get you to Doc Wilton,” I said as Travis veered in the direction of home. I grabbed his good arm and led him the opposite way. “I’ll stop at your folks house on my way home.”

“I’ll catch up to you after I get a head count,” Remy said.

With Travis in my care, I navigated him between the row of stores to the smaller homes where the shop owners and other professionals lived. Doc Wilton lived four houses down on the right, and I turned Travis in that direction, adjusting my pace to his.

“Thank you,” Travis whispered when we were far enough for Remy not to overhear.

I glanced at him and shrugged. “What was I going to do, leave your sorry butt out there on that bluff? I don’t think so.”

His smile wasn’t his usual bright grin. Instead, it seemed like forced bravery as he trudged towards the doctor’s house. His pale features set off my internal alarms, but I couldn’t force him to move any faster.

I had him lean against the wall next to the door while I knocked. The kindly gentleman opened the door, and his smile faded when his gaze landed on Travis. His grey eyes sharpened, and his hospitable mannerisms changed to all business, as he pushed open the screen door and waved us inside.

Doc Wilton's black salt and pepper hair belied his true age. He was young in comparison to Remy and Gram, but despite his youth, he was the best doctor in the region.

I remember seeing him for the first time the morning after I arrived in town. Gram wanted me to be checked out even though she couldn't find anything but stick scratches on me. Doc Wilton had just gotten out of medical school at some fancy faraway place, and had come back home to practice so his father could hang up his stethoscope.

I had been terrified and unable to stop shaking, and Gram was worried. She marched me across town to this very door. Doc Wilton's office smelled like rubbing alcohol and lemons and to this day, any time I smell a lemon, I drift back to his kind smile and calm demeanor.

As Travis and I crossed the threshold into his corner office, that scent assaulted my nose once again, creating a sense of calmness it always triggered. Like everything was going to be all right, despite Travis's current condition.

"You better get going before night falls," Doc Wilton said as he sat Travis on the exam table.

I traded a glance with Travis, and he gave me a nod. My grandmother's place was one of the few homes still surrounded by woodlands. She refused to pick up and leave, so while the majority of Dakota residents were within the town proper limits, we were still in the woods. The law of the land stated no one was to be wandering the woods after dark.

One look at the gloomy sky and my heart quickened. The light had dimmed enough to set off those damn alarms in my head, and I still had to stop at Travis's home to give his parents the news that he was at the doctor's.

I started back in the direction we had come in, briskly walking with purpose. When I turned into the alley Travis and I had come down, I bumped smack into Remy and nearly fell on my ass. If he hadn't grabbed me by the upper arms, I would have hit the dirt.

"You have to get home," he growled as he steadied me. His green eyes flashed with warning.

"I promised Travis I'd stop at his house and let his folks know where he is."

Remy's gaze rose to the sky, and he shook his head. "I'll take care of that. You need to get home before the sunlight fades. None of the parties encountered wolves today, so make sure to be vigilant."

He didn't need to say more. A howl came out of the south, echoing over the valley as if to punctuate his point. A shiver ran up my spine, and I gave him a nod.

He stepped around me heading towards Travis's home. "Get moving," he barked.

I obeyed his authoritative tone and turned on my heel. I sprinted towards home despite the protest in my already exhausted muscles. Swinging my bow off my shoulder, I approached the woods surrounding the town. The dark canopy swallowed me as I stepped into the forest with an arrow tightly set against my bow.

Twilight was the favored time of attack. The shadows along the path didn't help my pounding chest. I picked up my pace, ignoring the cramping in my calves and arms as I ran and kept my bow and arrow at the ready.

By the time I reached the cabin, dusk had settled in tight and my lungs burned from exertion.

I burst into the house expecting my grandmother to be standing over the stove cooking some delectable meal, but all that met me was the empty and silent cabin.

"Gram?" I called out as my heart thundered in my ears.

No answer.

I ran to her bedroom, hoping she would be in bed, but she was not in the cabin, and no increase in volume of calling her name was going to produce her from thin air. Heat engulfed me, and my breath caught in my lungs, forcing a wheeze. I stood back in the living room as my gaze darted around, looking for signs of what could have happened.

When my gaze landed on the empty spot where she usually kept her foraging basket and gloves, the lump in my throat plummeted. All the heat bled from my skin, and my teeth chattered.

She was still out there. I glanced at the dark woods, and a shiver grabbed hold of every cell. The last time I was in the forest at night, my family was slaughtered.

Chapter 5

THE WOODS ENVELOPED ME as I broke town law. If I was caught, I faced time in jail for this. But that wasn't what shook my muscles taut while my vision adjusted to the near blackness. I knew the path to the berry patch and the fruit orchard beyond like the back of my hand, but the shadows formed by the trees left my mouth dry and tinny.

I tried telling myself that my fear was keeping me vigilant, but I knew I was just fooling myself. The fright was making me jump at every noise to the point I was turning in frantic circles. I forced myself to stop and squat, taking each shaky breath until the quakes stopped.

Wolves can smell terror and if I didn't get myself back to center, my scent would surely drag their beastly asses in my direction. And wolves weren't the only threat in the forest. Wild cats and bears also ran in this neck of the wilderness, so I had to get my head together. Besides, I was already halfway to the berry patch and hadn't run across any signs of danger.

With a deep resolved breath, I climbed to my feet and continued my journey with as soft steps as I could take, making my focus the one-hundred-eighty-degree area in front of me. Stepping into the berry patch didn't bring me any comfort. I was nowhere near as good a tracker as Travis, but even in my sub-expert's eyes, the berry patch wasn't disturbed in a way that would indicate a struggle or even someone collapsing. Still, I navigated each row just in case.

At the far side of the berry patch, I turned, glancing at the woods surrounding the lush berries, looking for any sign that I was followed. Turning back to the orchards, I paused and closed my eyes, pulling whatever bravery I could from that well deep inside me.

I stepped towards the orchards with my bow at the ready. Traversing the orchard was a bit more difficult. My heart pumped pure adrenaline as I stepped out from tree to tree ready to let my arrow fly. It wasn't until the last row of trees that I found some spilled berries on the ground along with a snapped branch with an apple hanging on just by the barest of stems.

I tried to swallow as I stepped up to scan the steep slope under the moonlight, but the darkness at the bottom was impenetrable. Even under a high noon sun, the bottom of the hill is shadowed and dangerous to climb down.

I needed to backtrack around the side of the ledge to get to any point where I had solid footing right down to the valley floor. The candle I carried in my pocket wouldn't do any good in the gusty wind that had picked up with nightfall. I trotted to the middle of the berry patch and crossed into the narrow path that cut to the valley floor.

Concern braised my skin, overshadowing the fear tightening my core. I didn't bother with my bow and arrow until I was at the foot of the hill shrouded with night. The moonlight barely lit the valley floor. I glanced up, using the orchard tree line as a guide with my bow grasped tight.

I scanned the dark and sighed. I couldn't see, and I couldn't hold a lit candle while having my bow at the ready. If Gram fell, she would likely be hurt or worse. I slung the bow over my shoulder, digging the candle out along with the box of matches. I struck the match on the side of my pants. It caught the seam and flared to life.

With a candle leading the way, I held it low enough to avoid any sudden surge of air. The light illuminated a few feet at a time. I carefully planted my foot forward and turned, shielding the candle with my body as the light flickered.

I skirted around a boulder and froze at the sight of Gram's basket spilling bruised fruit on the ground. My gaze traveled farther beyond the basket.

The candle slipped from my fingers. I had an arrow threaded into my bow before the rush of air doused the flame. Dipped into sudden darkness, my chest felt like it would explode from the frantic beat of my heart. Sweat peppered my forehead, and hot beads dribbled down one of my temples.

Nothing moved. I squatted slowly, doubting myself. With one hand holding the arrow in place against the bow, I searched the ground for my light source. My fingers brushed the smooth wax and I grasped it tightly, working the blunt end into the dirt until it stood on its own. Then I struck another match and lit the wick.

I jumped to my feet, pulling the arrow taut. Wrapped around my grandmother was a massive grey wolf. The only shot I had was right between the beast's eyes. I lined up the shot, taking a slow breath before blowing a stream of air out between my lips.

The wolf opened his eyes, but didn't move. Those bright, crystal pearlescent blue eyes I remembered from my nightmares stared back at me. The beast's tongue flicked out, swiping my grandmother's cheek.

Gram moaned and I almost let the arrow sail, but I stalled when her soft voice whispered, "Ruby, stop."

The wolf's gaze was neither afraid nor angry. If read the creature right, it would have been compassion I saw, but I dismissed that as insane.

"Gram, move," I said through clenched teeth.

"No. Even if I could, I wouldn't. If this wolf hadn't come along, I would be dead now. He fought off another wolf and has kept me warm and safe since," she said.

My brain couldn't wrap around her words. All I saw was a monster, and what she said didn't make any sense. Every werewolf I had encountered operated on bloodlust. I shook my head, calculating the odds of being able to kill the beast, when part of her comment broke through the barrier in my mind.

"What do you mean by if you could move?"

"I'm hurt, dear," she said.

I lowered my bow but kept the arrow strung tight.

"Were you bitten?" The question squeezed from my throat.

Her eyes weren't luminescent like the wolf's, but that didn't mean anything. I had no idea how long the werewolf change took place if bitten. We always sacrificed the poor soul before they turned. I didn't know if I could kill my grandmother, even if she was poisoned by the beast.

"No," she said and her eyes closed. "No, I wasn't bitten. But I'm sure I broke a few things."

I glanced at the rocky terrain going up the hillside. I wouldn't have been surprised if she broke multiple things. If Travis shattered his arm from a ten-foot fall, it's a wonder my grandmother was able to speak.

"Put the bow and arrow away," Gram said. "And help me to my feet."

My gaze locked with the wolf's. If I put my weapon away, that would leave both of us vulnerable.

"Gram..."

"For heaven's sake, Ruby!"

Gram's angry hiss set me in motion. I stepped over the candle, creating enough of a breeze to blow the candle out. I muttered under my breath as my eyes took their sweet time adjusting to the blackness. The wolf's blue eyes became the only beacon I had, and they remained steady. Every cell in my body screamed danger as whatever remaining logic argued that the wolf could have killed both of us already.

His eyes flickered to my right and widened. I spun and let the arrow fly. A thud sounded. I flicked a match against the seam of my pants to see what the hell I hit. Another wolf lay a few feet behind me with my arrow embedded between its fading eyes.

I turned back to my grandmother and the beast that gave me enough of a warning to react. His eyes were locked back on me, but while his form had been relaxed before, it was now tense and broadcasting the same urgent message as that flashing under my skin.

We needed to get out of there. I dropped the match and closed the distance. Getting Gram to her feet wasn't easy, and her cry of pain when she applied pressure to her right leg sent a hot streak of panic through me. I glanced back the way I came at the dead carcass and then turned my gaze to the wolf now standing on the other side of my grandmother.

I took a step in the direction of home, and Gram made a muffled noise, gripping me tighter.

"I can't make it back in the dark," she whispered with a voice strained by pain. "We need to find someplace safe to hide until the sun rises."

I couldn't disagree, but the valley didn't have anywhere to hide. The wolf moved forward and stopped, looking back over his shoulder, his eyes bright orbs in the dark. When I didn't move, he came back and nudged me.

"I don't think so," I said, glaring at the massive wolf.

Holding on to my grandmother gave this beast the upper hand, and he could have gotten the jump on me. Instead, he nudged me again and trotted a few steps forward.

"I think he wants us to follow."

I knew the bastard wanted us to follow, but I couldn't figure out why. But being out here was just as dangerous, so I listened to my intuition and helped Gram hop on her good leg through the winding path.

The wolf kept looking back to make sure we were following, and he didn't wander ahead too far. But when he entered a thick canopy, I paused and my heart rate picked up. My grandmother's eyes were at half mast, and she looked much worse than Travis had earlier.

The wolf came back and peered out of the canopy at us. Instead of turning and leading, he came over to the other side of my grandmother, stepping close enough for her to cast her arm around his back for more support.

He swung his massive head in my direction and met my gaze. There was no malice evident in those blue eyes, but I still shivered with indecision.

"I think it's safe," Gram whispered.

I stepped into the dark woods, wondering if this would be the last thing I ever did.

Chapter 6

BEARING GRAM'S WEIGHT ON my already taxed muscles wasn't easy. I had to stop several times and shift her, and after trying to navigate the tight path, I knew there would have been no way I would have gotten her up the hill of the ravine and out of danger alone. The wolf bore an equal amount of Gram's weight, and there were several times that I thought about hauling her onto his back, but I didn't know whether that would be better or worse than walking. When we finally stepped into a large clearing, the moon had crossed the heavens and the constellations had shifted to a pattern I didn't recognize.

A small cottage sat in the center of the clearing. The wolf led us onto the porch and then pawed at the mat in front of the door until the corner folded back, revealing a key. I let Gram lean on the doorjamb and retrieved the key.

"Only my grandmother and I are going inside," I said and slid the key into the lock. With a twist of my wrist, the knob unlatched, and I helped Gram inside, closing the door on the wolf without any reservation.

I struck a match and found a lantern within reach. Lighting the wick produced a warm glow, and I blew the match out, setting it in the ceramic bowl next to the lantern. Nails clicked on the porch outside the door, and then a huff came as the wolf settled down to keep guard. I traded a glance with Gram and picked up the lantern as we headed across what looked like a family room into a hallway to find a bedroom and washroom at the end of the hall.

I got Gram situated in the bed and collapsed in the bedside chair, setting my bow and quiver within reach, just in case.

"Ruby," Gram started. "I'm not sure I'm going to make it."

A reprimand remained at the tip of my tongue. I closed my eyes, and taking a deep breath, I stood and pulled the covers back to make sure she didn't have the same type of fracture as Travis. I ignored Gram's gasps as I ran my hands down her side and leg, feeling my way in the low light. No bone stuck out of her skin, but I did feel the displacement in her hip as well as the weird angle in her thigh.

"You'll be fine," I said. "We just need to get you to Doc Wilton in the morning.

"I can't walk that far, honey."

"I know. I'll go get Midnight after sunrise."

"I can't ride in this condition," Gram muttered.

"I need to figure out what I'm going to do with that wolf," I said, trying to get Gram's mind off her injuries. My thoughts jumbled where the wolf was concerned. I knew my duty was to put the beast down, but he helped us, so my heart and my mind were now at odds.

"You can't be thinking what I think you're thinking," Gram said, her stern stare making me look away. "After all he did for us?"

"He's a werewolf." The statement hung on the air between us.

She crossed her arms and pursed her lips in anger. Red flared in her cheeks giving the rest of Gram's pale skin a more ghostly quality. I just shrugged.

"He isn't like the others," she whispered.

"I don't care." But I did, and it burned under the surface of my skin. My entire life I had seen those things as monsters to be destroyed, and then this beast showed compassion, kindness, and patience like he was human. It didn't settle well. "It's my job."

"It is not your job to become a monster," she hissed. "If you kill him, you will be no better than the rest of the beasts taking innocent lives."

I leaned back in the chair. Her words were as effective as a slap across the face, and they stung just as deeply. I didn't want to believe that any of the werewolves were capable of good, but I couldn't deny what this one had done for us. It was a paradox.

"How do you know he's innocent?"

Her crossed arms loosened and she sighed. "I don't know if he is innocent or not. But I do know he could have torn me to pieces or let the other wolf that came along right before he did. He chased it off and came back, offering me his warmth despite my condition. He also tensed and then relaxed after you killed that other wolf, which may have been the same one he chased off earlier."

"Maybe he was just protecting his meal," I said, but it didn't ring true in my ears.

Gram scoffed and waved her hand at me. The movement caused her to grimace.

"Get some rest," I said and blew out the lantern, dousing us in darkness.

The waxing moon shone through the side window. In less than a week it would be full. I closed my eyes, trying to get some rest, but my mind kept racing, kept turning over what I needed to do when the night was through.

I had already broken the curfew, and for that I'd be facing jail time if anyone found out. Letting a werewolf live had an entirely different punishment, one that would have me facing a jury of my peers and a potential death sentence.

Chapter 7

I JERKED AWAKE AND wiped the drool from my cheek. Another clang from the outer room had me on my feet with the bow threaded with an arrow. Gram still slept, her pale face visible above the comforter. I crept towards the door, padding as silently as I could while every nerve ending pulsed. I opened the bedroom door and glanced down the hall into the brightly lit family room area. The front door was still closed, but the distinct sound of someone inside the cabin filtered to my ears.

I crossed the distance and pointed my bow in the direction of the kitchen. Heat danced on my skin as I stared at the chiseled back of a man standing over the stove. His hair was jet black, matching the color of the pants he wore, and every movement he made rippled through the muscles in his back. When he glanced over his shoulder with the same piercing blue eyes the wolf had last night, heat engulfing me moved lower into my belly.

"Shoot if you have to," he said and turned back to the stove. "But it would be a shame to ruin breakfast."

Even his voice tickled the triggers inside me. It was deep and musical and almost hypnotic. I had never heard a werewolf's voice, only the howls and growls from the beasts.

The man turned with a pan in his hands and dumped scrambled eggs on the two plates sitting on the small table.

"How did you get in?" I asked and cursed the breathless quality of my voice. I still held the arrow tight on the bow.

He smiled and I nearly fell to my knees at the small dimples in his cheeks and the playful shine in his eyes. "There's more than one way to get into this house." He turned his back and put the pan into a wash basin before taking a seat at the table. "Eat. Then you can kill me."

I lowered the bow and stared at him as he began eating the eggs in front of him. I knew I should put him down, but there was something disarming about the man, and I could not bring myself to shoot him. Frustration gathered inside me, along with something more primal, and I gave in to the civility of the moment.

I sat, but kept the bow and arrow within reach in case the wolf attacked.

"Where did you get the eggs?" I asked, assuming he had stolen them.

"My henhouse out back." He hooked his thumb over his shoulder. "And the milk came from the cows." He pointed to the glass in front of me.

My fork stalled on the way to my mouth, and I just stared at the man. There was no precedence for a werewolf having a farm. At least not one where animals lived long enough to produce food.

He smiled. "Eat up before your eggs get cold, then we can check on your grandmother."

My muscles remembered what they were doing, and I took my first bite. The scrambled eggs were good. Not runny or rubbery, but just right. I focused on feeding my growling stomach.

I hadn't realized how hungry I was, but then again, adrenaline kept me moving last night, so my lack of a meal didn't hit until now.

I finished every kernel on the plate and gave him an awkward smile of gratitude.

He stood, cleared the plates, and proceeded to wash the dishes while I sat dumbfounded.

"Who are you?" I finally asked.

He turned towards me while wiping his hands on a dishtowel. "Lucas Bayo," he said and stepped towards me.

I reacted and strung the arrow in the bow, jumping to my feet as shock and panic filled my muscles. My gaze dropped to his extended hand, and a hot flush filled my cheeks. He was just being polite and offering a handshake. I closed my eyes and sighed.

"I'm sorry, but I don't trust you enough to let my guard down," I said and stepped backwards. "My parents were killed by your kind and..."

He pulled his hand back and slid it in his pocket. "My kind." His voice filled with bitterness, and he nodded like he understood my reaction. "Well, then, you do what you need to do." He leaned against the sink, his expression resolved but not fearful.

I pointed the arrow at him and pulled it back. The tip centered on his chest, but my gaze locked with his. That primal urge to drop the bow and arrow and jump into his arms filled my form. I wanted those full lips on mine, those strong hands cupping my...

"Damn it," I muttered, shaking the inappropriate thoughts from my head. The fabric of my vest rubbed against my breasts in a way that was both uncomfortable and just as arousing as looking into Lucas's eyes. I lowered my bow. "How many humans have you killed?"

"None."

I stared at him and relaxed my grip on the bow and arrow, but didn't put it away. Not just yet.

"You expect me to believe that?"

"I really don't care what you believe. It's the truth, and you can take it or leave it."

His arms crossed, making the muscles in his chest flex in a way that made me shift to try to quell the heat pooling between my legs. I didn't know what the hell had gotten into me, but I couldn't bring myself to kill him. Not with my grandmother's words still ringing in my head. I unthreaded my arrow and dropped it back in my quiver.

"If you so much as twitch the wrong way, I'll kill you."

He gave me a huff of a laugh and dropped his arms. "Can we go see how your grandmother is doing?"

"Fine." I waved for him to lead the way.

Lucas rolled his eyes and headed towards the bedroom, his gait that of someone who wasn't at all happy with the situation. It amused me, but my amusement died as soon as the door opened.

Gram's pale features set my heart on overdrive. The bow fell from my fingers, hitting the floor as I skidded to a stop by her side. Her eyes opened at the sound, and she blinked at Lucas standing a few feet away. Her gaze moved to mine, and she formed a smile.

"I guess I've made it through the night." Gram's weak voice came out in a whisper.

"Yes." Lucas stepped around me and put his wrist to her forehead. He glanced at me with sadness in his eyes. "She needs a doctor. Today."

I nodded. "I need to get my horse."

"I've got one that we can use," he said.

"I can get my horse," I said, straightening my back.

"Look, there is no time for you to travel to Dakota and back. She needs to be transported now, not tomorrow."

"I won't bring anyone back with me if that is what you're worried about," I snapped.

He raised his eyebrows. "I'm not worried about a hunting party. I'm worried about whether your grandmother will make it back alive. And I am not taking her through the woods at night. That's a death wish waiting to happen no matter how good you are with that bow and arrow."

The growl in his voice caught me as off guard as his words.

"I don't think I can ride," Gram said, her voice frail.

"It's okay. You can ride on my lap so you don't get jostled as much." Lucas turned to me. "My mare is out in the barn. I'm assuming you know how to put a saddle on."

I cocked my head and narrowed my eyes. "I'll stay with my grandmother while you go prepare the horse."

"Do you know how to splint a leg?" he asked.

I shifted and nodded, but that wasn't true.

"For heaven's sake, Ruby, go get the horse ready," Gram scolded.

I glanced at her and then at Lucas. Pointing my finger, I opened my mouth.

"I know. If I harm her in any way, I'm a dead man," he cut in.

I swiped my bow off the ground and stormed out of the room while my grandmother apologized for my rash behavior. The last thing I heard before I stepped out the door was Lucas saying I was entitled to my feelings. As unsettled as I was about leaving Gram with him, I was also curious to see what his land truly held.

I made my way to the side of the house and gawked at the barn and the surrounding farmlands. Wooden fences gated the animals as well as the gardens starting at the back of the house. Just beyond the perimeter fence was the forest. I couldn't imagine keeping the farm safe from the dangers in the woods. Not only were there werewolves, but there were plenty of other predators looking for an easy meal.

Lucas Bayo was one big mystery, and as I unhooked the gate and passed through to the pasture, I realized I wanted to unravel the layers and get to the core of the man. A heat burned deep inside me, one that had never been lit before, and I cursed under my breath.

Lucas was a werewolf.

The thought pounded my brain with each step. I couldn't let this weird attraction take over and cloud my mind. When Gram was back home under the care of the doctor, I would honor my oath and do my duty, even if it killed me.

One bite and he could create an army to overrun Dakota.

I opened the barn door and scanned the interior. Chickens pecked their way across the interior and the hen house lined the wall to my left while stalls filled the right side of the barn. Most of the stalls were empty, but two had occupants. One held a milking cow and the other a horse.

"Focus," I mumbled and approached the old mare that reminded me of a bowl of cinnamon sugar. White and brown speckled her coat, and she whinnied as I approached.

"It's okay, girl," I said softly and reached for the reins on the wall.

I stepped to the stall door and gently ran my hand down her nose and to the side of her jaw. She sniffed my hand, looking for a treat, and then met my gaze. For a minute there, I saw a shadow of our old mare who carried me to that fateful clearing all those years ago, but the vision passed just as quick.

The horse allowed me to fit her bit and strap on the reins without any fuss, and I led her out of the stall. She patiently stood while I threw her saddle blanket in place and fit the saddle on tight. I led her to the post just outside the back of the house and descended a stairwell to a door.

The knob turned easily to Lucas's root cellar. This must have been how he got inside the house this morning. The stairs led up to the door across from the bedroom. I closed the door and glanced at the knob. I engaged the lock and strode towards the bedroom.

My grandmother moaned.

It was as if lightning shot through my veins. I had the bow and arrow in my grasp before my brain caught up to what I was seeing. Lucas was wrapping my grandmother's thigh in gauze. Along her outer thigh and hip, he had placed a piece of sturdy lumber that went from her hip all the way down to her knee. Smaller pieces framed her upper and inner thigh, and from the way he was moving her, I would guess there was another piece of wood framing the back of her leg.

Sweat poured from her face. Each time Lucas rolled the gauze under her leg, she whined. He kept apologizing each time he had to move her, and finally he tied the bandage off just above the knee and turned towards me.

"This is going to be a rough ride," he said, his eyes relaying a world of concern.

"I can take care of her," I said, ignoring the pang that went through me.

"I'm going with you two," he said.

I laughed at him. There was no hiding his pearlescent eyes. The town would string him up with silver and slowly torture him to death. I shook my head. "No. They will kill you on sight."

"*You* didn't."

I opened my mouth to speak, but I couldn't find the words. Alarms were already ringing in my head. "You can't come," I finally squeaked out.

"She's right. They won't understand," Gram said.

Lucas ran his hand through his thick hair and crossed to his bureau. He pulled on a shirt much to my dismay and then offered me one. "It's colder today than it was yesterday."

I glanced down at my vest, and heat filled my cheeks. I had totally forgotten I lent my shirt to Travis. I had been so preoccupied at my surroundings that I didn't notice how cold it was. I almost declined, but Gram's raised brow made me take the shirt and retreat as quickly as possible from the room.

In the washroom, I slid the shirt over my head. The material was soft and hung over my small form. I tucked the hem into my pants and slid my vest back on. I had to roll up the sleeves to almost my elbows in order to not get in the way of my bow and arrow if the need arose.

I stepped back in the room a few minutes later, and Gram gave me that same raised brow.

"Travis fell from a tree and needed a sling. Remy had already used his shirt sleeves for a splint, so I was the last one left with a shirt." Heat engulfed my entire face, and I glanced at the floor. This wasn't a conversation I wanted to have in front of a stranger. A sexy stranger at that. A sexy werewolf, my mind corrected. He pulled on his boots, and my gaze fell to the open *V* of his shirt and the firm, smooth skin peeking out of his tunic.

"So you gave the shirt off your back to help a friend?" His bright blue eyes met mine.

"I guess," I answered.

The dimples in his cheeks toyed with my insides. He stood and crossed to the spot in front of me, his gaze never leaving mine. "I can't let you try to make this trip with just your grandmother. That wolf you killed last night, that wasn't the only one in the area."

"Your horse can't hold all three of us."

"Yes, she can."

I knew there were more wolves out there. A whole pack, but I didn't want to be responsible for this creature's death. "Lucas, they will kill you," I said slowly, enunciating every word to make my point.

His easy smile burned through me. "Then you won't have to make that call." He slid into his coat, pulling the hood over his head, scooped Gram up in his arms, and headed out the front door.

I followed and brought the mare around front where Lucas hopped on with Gram in his arms, shifting her until she was as comfortable as possible. He offered me his hand, and I swatted it away. Using the porch, I climbed onto the back half of the saddle and wrapped my right arm around his waist.

"I'll do what I can to keep you comfortable, but you and I both know time isn't on our side right now," Lucas said to my grandmother.

She nodded.

He glanced back at me. "Hold on," he said and then kicked his heels into the horse.

The mare took off like a bolt that belied her calm demeanor. She reminded me of Midnight as she traversed through the woods. I clung to Lucas and my bow, wondering if Gram felt every hoof beat or not. Her pale, stressed features worried me.

Her eyes met mine. She offered me a grimace instead of a smile, but just the effort alone was endearing.

“Werewolf coming fast on the right.” Lucas’s purr reached my ears.

I tightened my thighs and swung the bow in that direction, threading it with an arrow as we rode through the thick woods. The mare never slowed down or veered from her path. I caught the flash of the wolf’s iridescent eyes just as it launched into the air.

My arrow pierced right through its head. Lucas sent a punch in its direction so the dead beast wouldn’t knock us off the horse. His strength and calmness astounded me, and for a moment, I allowed myself to be in awe of the man regardless of the beast inside.

I repositioned myself and wrapped my right arm around his waist again, hugging him tight as we continued at breakneck speed.

Chapter 8

THE MID-AFTERNOON SUN DIDN'T offer much warmth, and I shivered as I slid off the horse in front of Doc Wilton's. I knocked on the door, and when it swung open, Doc Wilton's kind smile disappeared. He opened the door, waving us inside.

We hurried through the house to Doc Wilton's office where Lucas laid Gram on the exam table.

“I did my best to try to keep her broken bones stable on the ride...” he said and stepped back. “I think she may be bleeding internally.”

The doctor snapped his gaze to Lucas as if seeing him for the first time. His eyes narrowed before he grabbed a pair of scissors and started cutting through the gauze.

“You did fine,” Gram whispered to Lucas and stretched her hand out for me.

I stepped to her side and took it.

“Get him somewhere safe,” she whispered.

Doc Wilton looked up from his task. “Why would you let that monster near your grandmother?”

“He saved me, Jacob,” Gram said. “I was stupid and tried to use the berm to grab an apple off a high limb and lost my balance. I fell all the way into the valley gorge. He came around just when another wolf found me. He protected me, running that varmint off, and then curled around me to keep me warm. When Ruby found us, he kept both of us safe through the night. He didn’t have to help us at all. And he certainly didn’t need to risk his life by coming here, so you just hush up and leave him be.”

Doc Wilton looked down as pink bloomed in his cheeks. “Yes, Mrs. Locklear.” He slowly removed the outer splint, and Gram groaned through clenched teeth. He glanced up at us. “Go home. I’ll come get you when she is stable.”

Gram squeezed my hand and then let go, giving me a reassuring smile. When I didn’t move, she turned her gaze to Lucas. “Have her take you to our cottage. You should be safe there until nightfall.”

Lucas nodded. “Yes, ma’am.”

“Ruby, don’t let anything happen to him, okay?”

I rolled my eyes and nodded. “Fine.” I took a second to give her a hug. “I love you, Gram,” I whispered.

“I love you, too, child. Now go, before the Guard gets back.” She met my gaze with a clear warning in her eyes.

I knew I’d have to face Remy later today when the Guard got home, but if he intercepted us on the way home, Lucas would not get out of Dakota alive. I gave her a nod and stepped outside with Lucas.

Without a word, he lifted me onto the mare and hopped on behind me. He handed me the reins.

“Lead the way,” he said and gently banged his heels against the mare’s sides.

She started trotting as I led her through the back side of the village and into the woods.

"You don't live in town?" he asked as we went deeper down the secondary path that I rarely traveled.

"No. Gram has always lived outside the town proper." I turned the mare to our left, doubling back to the stables behind our cottage. Our clearing was tiny in comparison to Lucas's land, but it was all we had.

We didn't have issues with predators either, but that was due to the wolf carcasses hanging on every post. Lucas tensed as I stopped at the gate. I slid off the horse and took the reins, leading the horse through to the inside of the corral with Lucas still on her back. The gate closed behind us, and he twitched in the seat. His gaze passed over each pelt before dropping to mine.

His teeth peeled back in horror at the vulgar display of death.

"It keeps Midnight safe." I nodded to the black stallion drinking from the trough. "I don't know what you did around yours, but this works like a charm." I waved at the perimeter.

Lucas huffed and climbed off the horse. "I marked the territory. You've announced death to all who enter." He nodded at the posts. "No werewolf in their right mind would breach that line."

"And yet you are standing inside my perimeter." I cocked an eyebrow.

"I never professed to be of the right mind," he said and took the reins of the horse, leading her towards the water trough.

Midnight reacted as he got closer. My stallion's nose flared and he neighed, shaking his head before he reared on his hind legs.

"Cool your hide," Lucas said to Midnight. "My girl needs some water." He led the mare to the water and stood between his horse and Midnight.

Midnight stomped his hoof and backed away. He didn't like the presence of a werewolf in his domain, and he trotted over to me, nudging me away from Lucas until I captured his head between my hands.

"Middy, it's okay. He isn't going to hurt us. I promise." My calm voice seemed to do the trick, but my horse wanted nothing to do with either the mare or Lucas.

Lucas took the saddle and blanket off and placed them in the shed with my other riding equipment. He took off the mare's bridle and bit and hung that up beside Midnight's before he stepped out and nodded towards the cabin.

"Do you mind if we go inside? This is kind of unsettling." He twirled his finger around to indicate my safeguards.

His discomfort amused me. So did the fact that he could just throw me over his shoulder and take me inside instead of being so polite. I gave him a nod and headed towards the back door.

He followed and once inside, his entire body seemed to melt with relief. He leaned against the door.

"You're that girl, aren't you?" he asked while looking at the ceiling.

He said *that girl* in the same tone I used when I said *his kind* this morning. When his gaze dropped to mine, I shivered.

"You're the legendary wolf killer that I keep hearing about."

I smiled and shrugged. "I guess."

His eyes closed again, and he took a deep breath that expanded his chest. "There is a price on your head." He straightened and walked past me directly to the ice box in the kitchen.

"What are you doing?" I asked when I rounded the corner.

"I'm hungry and I was looking at what you had available."

"That's our food," I said.

He shot a glare in my direction. "I shared my breakfast with you." He pulled out a slice of venison from under the ice and held it up. "Do you mind if I cook this up?"

I bit my lip for a second feeling a bit selfish. I thought about what Gram would want me to do. She would want me to be the perfect host to our guest, but I wasn't willing to go that far. If he wanted to cook, by all means, he could cook.

"Go ahead. I'm going to clean up." I turned, hanging my bow and quiver on the hooks in the hallway as a sign of trust. I still had my silver blade if he decided I was worth the bounty, but I didn't think he'd go through all this trouble in the name of collecting on my head.

I filled the tub with lukewarm water and stripped my clothing. I stepped into the water and sat, sucking my breath in at the coolness of the bath. If I had been a little more patient, the water would have been hot enough to not shiver as I scrubbed the dirt from my skin. When I finished with my body, I dunked my head under the water and shook it, hoping that would be enough to clean the dirt from my braid.

The scent of food drifted under the door, and my stomach responded with a growl. I climbed out and toweled off before dumping the dirty water out the window. I'd have to fill the warmer with wood chips and the pot with water later, but right now, I was hungry.

I wrapped the towel around me and gathered my clothes. I'd have to do the wash in another day, but for now, I'd put on something comfortable instead of my hunting pants and vest. I pulled open the door, and Lucas stood right outside with his hand poised to knock.

His eyes flickered as his gaze dropped from my face to the towel hiding my endowments. His cheeks flared red as his eyes found mine again. "Um, dinner is ready." He backed away, giving me just enough room to scoot by him.

Just being in close proximity to him turned my skin into an inferno, and I hurried into my bedroom, shutting the door on his curious gaze. I leaned against the wood and stared up at the ceiling, asking for strength. As a member of the Guard, I could not fall for a wolf no matter how attractive he was.

With a deep breath and a slow exhale, my skin cooled. I pulled on undergarments, stockings, my hunting dress, and boots. It was much less comfortable than my nightshirt, but I wasn't going to make myself vulnerable with a stranger in the house.

I stepped out into the living area, and Lucas was sitting at the table waiting for me. Both our plates were brimming with venison, and a half loaf of bread sat sliced between them.

"Thank you," I said and took the seat opposite him.

"You're welcome." He focused on the food in front of him.

For a lone werewolf, he seemed to have impeccable manners. When he finally looked up, his cheeks flared red.

"What?" he asked.

"I'm just surprised you have manners," I mumbled and cut another piece of perfectly cooked venison. I also did not want to admit to him that he was a better cook than I was. My venison usually came out like rawhide, but this came out as good as Gram made it.

"I was brought up by my mother. My human mother," he said. "She taught me how to act with other people, and despite my father's barbaric ways, her teachings stuck with me. I am not like the other beasts out there." He nodded towards the window. "I was born this way."

I stared at him with a raised eyebrow. "What do you mean?"

"I am the only werewolf that I know of that was birthed by a human. Even the original was changed by an ancient rite and not by birth. I also don't have the same bloodlust as my kind. It's the reason I'm on their bounty list, too."

I didn't realize I had stopped with my fork halfway to my mouth until he cocked his head at me. Heat flushed my face, and I dropped my gaze to my plate. "So, you're an outlaw?"

He laughed. "Certainly to humans, but that's because they don't stop to question whether killing me is just or not. They assume my heritage makes me a killer, which is incorrect. I am half human and half wolf and have always refused to attack people. I have never bitten anyone either because I have no idea what kind of curse I would be passing on. Because I refused to kill humans or attempt to turn them, I lost my family."

My eyes softened.

His lips tightened. "I have killed, though. The day they killed my mother, I tore the pack to pieces. So, I've committed the ultimate sin in the eyes of the werewolf clan." He shrugged and went back to eating his meal.

A lump formed in the back of my mouth as a deep sadness filled me. Lucas had no one. Humans didn't trust him, and his own kind hunted him. I cleared my throat and focused on my food. Before I had a chance to finish, a knock on the front door interrupted us.

Adrenaline rushed through me as I stared at Lucas. His back was towards the door, but if anyone saw a stranger eating in my grandmother's home, there would be hell to pay. I pointed to the kitchen, and he picked up his plate and moved to the corner near the sink, which was a blind spot to the front door.

I waited a second and then cracked the door. Annie Wilton stood on the threshold, with Doc Wilton's horse tied to the front porch post. My heart thundered in my chest at the stricken look on her face.

"There were complications. Come quickly," she said and grabbed my hand, pulling me out the door.

I took one glance at Lucas, and he nodded before the door closed on his worried gaze. My stomach dropped because I was certain I would come home to an empty house, but my grandmother's situation was more pressing than Lucas's. I hopped onto the back of Doc's horse without prompting, and Annie kicked its sides. We were galloping at top speed within a few breaths.

When the horse skidded to a stop a few minutes later at Doc Wilton's house, I hopped off and ran into the house without a glance back at Annie.

Gram was strapped onto the same exam table I had left her on. However, she looked much worse now. Her skin had turned to grey and her lips almost blue. My gaze dropped to the floor. To the mess of red towels and rags.

Gram moved her hand, and I stepped close to take it. She tried to speak, but all that came out was a harsh rasp. I leaned close.

"Love you, Ruby," she whispered.

I pulled away. "I love you, too, Gram," I said, and it was as if my words pulled the last of the air from her lungs.

Her raspy breath stopped on an exhale. I waited for her to inhale again.

"Gram?" I squeezed her hand. "Gram?" The pounding in my ears drowned out all sound. I shook her arm. "Gram!"

Doc Wilton moved behind me and clasped my shoulders, trying to pull me away from my grandmother.

I spun around to face him. "You have to help her!"

"I can't. That's why I sent Annie to get you. Your grandmother lost too much blood. Her hip shattered and punctured an artery in several places. It was a miracle she remained as lucid as she did for so long. There was nothing I could do." He ran his hand through his hair. "There was just too much damage."

"You can't help her?" I asked with a voice I didn't recognize. "You can't save her?"

"No, honey. She's already gone. She held on to say her goodbye to you."

Tears blurred my vision, and my throat closed against the wail of sorrow filling my soul. The last of my family lay on that table, and my heart broke with the loss. My knees wobbled, but I wouldn't allow them to buckle.

Not here.

Not in front of her spirit.

Gram would expect me to be strong, to carry on without her, but all I wanted to do was curl up in a ball and forget the world around me. I pressed my lips together and turned, taking one last glance at the woman who raised me to be strong and independent.

"Bye, Gram," I whispered and turned towards the door.

"I'll make the arrangements," Doc Wilton said.

I nodded and left his house as fog filtered through my brain. Memories of Gram's laughter and her gumption flashed in front of my eyes. I didn't remember the walk to the cabin, but I found myself staring at the door with arms that were too heavy to lift.

After a moment, the door cracked open, and Lucas's bright blue eyes peered out at me. A wave of relief hit, and my chin quivered. He opened the door wider and closed it as I crossed the threshold. Gratitude that I wasn't alone in Gram's house layered on the sorrow. Without permission, tears flowed hot from my eyes, streaking my cheeks.

My knees buckled and I dropped, hitting the floor with a dull thud. Lucas's shadow crossed over mine, and his hand cupped my shoulder as he crouched down next to me. His kind eyes triggered the gates, and a sob slipped from my lips. I covered my face to try to quiet the horrible sounds.

Lucas pulled me onto his lap. His arms wrapped around me, offering warmth and comfort. He didn't bother with meaningless words. He let me purge the pain onto his shoulder in a wealth of tears until his shirt was as wet as my face. When I finally quieted down, he stood with me in his arms and brought me to my bedroom. After he laid me on the bed and slid my boots off, he covered me with a blanket and glanced at the window.

"The sun is setting," he said, and hooked his thumb over his shoulder.

"Stay," I whispered. My request was more for his safety, but I also didn't want to be alone.

"People are going to come by," he said.

I huffed. “Not at night. No one is allowed outside after dark.” They would be here first thing in the morning, but while the darkness blanketed the woods, no one in their right mind wandered.

He blinked at me and gave me a half smile. “So you defied town ordinances by searching for your grandmother last night?”

“Yes. That comes with jail time. But having you here...” I shrugged. There was no use telling him I was facing a death sentence if anyone found out I allowed him to live.

Reality slammed home. I put Doc Wilton in the same position as I now sat in. I closed my eyes and buried my face in the pillow because I didn’t want to entertain what Doc would do now that Gram had died.

Lucas lit the lamp on my nightstand and then started for the door.

“Where are you going?”

He stopped and shifted from foot to foot as he looked out the window. “I need to go.”

I glanced at the darkened window and then back at him.

“Damn it,” he muttered and doubled over before falling to his knees.

All my sorrow and every narration in my head halted as his gaze locked on mine. His eyes flared bright. I blinked as the fabric encasing him tore, the sound of it sending a shiver up my spine. His hands clenched into tight fists as the cords on his neck stood out. His muscles trembled hard enough for me to feel it in the springs of the bed.

The transformation from man to massive wolf did not look pleasant in the least. It wasn't done in a snap, where one moment he was a man and the next he was a wolf, like I always assumed. Bones cracked and stuck out at odd angles while he silently endured the pain. There was a final snap, and then the wolf looked at me amidst the ruined clothing.

He glanced at the mess surrounding him and sighed before using his snout and front paw to bundle up the scraps into a small pile that he picked up and brought over to the trashcan in the corner.

Questions surfaced, but I wouldn't get any answers until morning. Lucas curled up in the corner and put his massive head on his paws. I stared at him in silence until my eyelids dropped closed, and I let the exhaustion claim me.

Chapter 9

KNOCKING INTERUPPTED MY BROKEN dreams. I rolled away from the noise, curling into a tighter ball and shivering against the morning chill.

"Ruby?"

The strange voice penetrated my sleep-addled brain. My eyes flew open, landing on a bare chest on the opposite side of the bed. I sat up and glanced down at my attire, and then everything fell into place. This wasn't a nightmare after all.

I stared at Lucas. He stood wrapped from the waist down in the comforter, and what was visible was a sculpted torso like I had never seen before. I wanted to reach out and touch the relief map of his chest and feel the muscles under my fingertips. Another shiver captured me, and I wrapped my arms around my stocking-clad legs.

"Someone is here," he said and nodded towards the bedroom door.

The knocking continued, and I climbed out of the bed.

"Just stay in here," I said before I left the room.

"If you get the chance to grab the saddle bag I slung over the fence out back, I have an extra pair of clothes in there," he said.

"I'll do my best." I closed the bedroom door and crossed to the front door.

Outside stood the entire squad, led by Remy. His solemn features and reddened eyes told me more than I wanted to know about how he felt about Gram. He gave me a nod and went to step inside.

I blocked his path. The last thing I needed was the Guard milling about while I had a naked werewolf in my bedroom.

"Remy, I really don't want any company right now. I'm sorry, but I need some time to let this all sink in," I said and glanced at the twenty men standing outside.

His face hardened, and his eyes narrowed. "You went looking for her after dark, didn't you?" His voice turned as fiery as his glare.

There was no sense in denying it, so I nodded. "It was Gram." My chin trembled and my eyes filled with hot tears, but I blinked them back and started to close the door on the group.

"Doc said you had help."

I stared at him. "Yes. A farmer from outside Dakota territory found us and helped me get Gram to Doc's office."

Remy gave a slow nod.

"Gram would have died out in the woods otherwise," I said and my voice cracked. "Lot of good it did anyways." I shut the door before the tears came in earnest.

"You know where to find us if you need anything," Remy said and patted the door a couple times.

“Thank you,” I called out.

Footsteps shuffled away. When I no longer heard noise, I opened the door just to check. No one was in sight. I shut the door and hurried out the back and into the corral. Lucas’s saddle bag hung by the stable, and I ran across the field and grabbed it.

Back in the house, I tossed the bag into my bedroom and closed the door, leaning my back on it for a moment to get my racing heart under control. I closed my eyes and concentrated on my breathing, slowing it down until I almost felt normal. When I opened my eyes, my gaze landed on my grandmother’s room. A lump returned to my throat.

I would not be able to escape her within the confines of these walls.

The bedroom door opened, and I jumped and spun around, right into Lucas’s bare chest. His skin was warm and soft, and I pushed off with my hands, taking a step back. His eyes were as wide as mine as we stared at each other.

Another knock at the door broke whatever spell had captivated us. I glanced at the front of the house and then at Lucas.

“You need a shirt,” I mumbled under my breath.

A smile toyed on his lips. “I don’t have one,” he whispered.

My gaze dropped to the rocking chair where my pile of clothes from yesterday sat and I pointed. “Yes, you do.”

He turned and I swore his shoulders dropped a fraction as if he were as disappointed as I was for him to cover up. I crossed to quell the knocking at the front door.

Travis stood on the other side of the threshold, his face still on the pale side. His arm was set in a plaster cast and held in a much more stable sling than my shirt. He gave me a tired smile and handed me my soiled shirt.

“I’m sorry to hear about your grandmother,” he said.

I pressed my lips together and nodded, blinking away the mist that blurred my vision. He stepped towards me, but I put my hand out, stopping him.

“I’m okay,” I said, but my shaky voice belied my words. I silently cursed at my inability to stabilize my emotions.

“You’re about as okay as I am,” he said and raised an eyebrow.

It never occurred to me that anyone else would have a big empty space in the middle of their chest like I had, but on closer inspection, Travis's eyes were more bloodshot than normal. It wasn't cold enough outside to warrant the redness on the end of his nose that matched the lines traversing his eyes.

Anyone just glancing at him would have surmised he had been tossing whiskey back all night at the local pub. But I knew better. I knew what those signs meant in my best friend. He hadn't been able to curb his sorrow, either.

He pointed his chin at the inside of the cabin. "Are you going to just stand there, or are you going to let me in?"

"I'm not up for company," I said and felt about as good as a piece of horse dung about that.

"That's what Remy said when I passed the group." He stepped closer as if he was going to pass my body blockade.

I put my arm up against the door jamb, stopping him dead.

Travis sent a sideways glance at me. The crease between his eyes was deep enough to broadcast his irritation.

"Are you serious?" He straightened his back and glared. "Do you think you're the only one grieving?"

I opened my mouth to reply, but I didn't have any comeback that wouldn't hurt him more than he looked. It wasn't like him to get angry with me, either. I shook my head and stepped aside so he could enter.

"I'm sorry. I'm just not in the mood for anyone to be here," I said and closed the door.

Travis took a seat on the couch. "I'm not just anyone."

He was my best friend after all, and even though he had delusions of a future with me, I couldn't deny he had always been there when I needed him. If Lucas hadn't been in the next room, I probably would have had a house full of people offering condolences and casseroles, and he would have been at my side fending people off so I could have some peace.

"I know." I turned away and headed into the kitchen to keep myself preoccupied. I couldn't pass off the thundering of my heart or the heated flush now filling my form as mourning. If I stayed by the hearth, Travis would soon figure out something else was digging at my nerves more than my grandmother passing.

I stared at the jar of Gram's cookies.

A hand on my arm pulled a yelp from me and I spun, staring at Travis with wide eyes. I hadn't heard him cross the room.

“You haven’t heard a word I said.”

I shook my head.

“Have you picked out your grandmother’s final resting clothing?”

I recoiled at his words, stepping back like he had produced a rotten tomato. It was as if he’d yanked the hurt right back to the surface where it burned. I didn’t want to pick out the clothes she would be buried in. I wanted her burned and her ashes spread on the four winds like we had always talked about.

“Gram didn’t want to be buried,” I said. “Neither one of us want to be put in a pine box in the ground.”

He arched his brow. “You still need to provide the doctor with clothing, and then they will bring your grandmother to the church for viewing.”

I stared at him, my brain unable to comprehend what he was saying. “I thought they’d bring Gram back here?” At least that was the custom I was used to in this town. Calling hours happened at the home of the deceased. As far back as I can remember, Gram and I would walk into town to pay our respects and then come back home until the burial. But in this case, I had promised Gram I would burn her remains after the calling hours and just have a headstone which held up the pretense of her being buried. Now, I’d never get the chance to do what she expected me to. The only bodies that were cremated were those that were riddled with disease. Burning a non-diseased body was frowned upon and thought of as blasphemous.

"You live all the way out here," he mumbled and stared at his feet. "I can take whatever you'd like back to the doctor so he can get your grandmother ready."

"Wrap her in cheese cloth and douse her in kerosene. She wants to ride the winds to wherever God chooses to plant her ashes. She never wanted to be stuck in a box in the cold hard ground."

"You know that isn't right," he started.

My glare shut him up. "Have them bring Gram here. I'll take care of her."

"Red, they aren't going to do that. Both the doctor and the priest insisted on having the services in town. Your grandmother was loved by every single person in this village, and they want to honor her."

"No, they don't. They don't want to honor her wishes. They want to do what they feel is proper. And so do you. Just go tell them to bring her body back here!" I yelled and pointed at the door.

Travis turned and headed down the hallway into uncharted territory. Before I could stop him, he pushed open the first door on the right. My bedroom. Where Lucas was hiding.

Travis froze in place with his mouth ajar and his good hand still flat on the wood. The creak of springs followed.

"Who the hell..." he started and then took a quick step backwards into the far wall, his eyes even wider than before. "What the..." His gaze landed on my quiver a few feet away.

Before I could move, he had an arrow in his hand and charged into my room holding the thing like a dagger. I was on his heels in a flash, but not before he struck out at Lucas.

Lucas parried, knocking Travis's good arm away, but the sizzle of silver on skin and a burning stench filled the room.

"Travis, stop!"

He was nearly feral with his lips peeled back and a snarling growl coming from his throat. I would have thought the beast in the room was my best friend, not the man trying to defend himself against a silver arrow.

Travis got a few licks in before Lucas grabbed the shaft and snapped the wood, tossing the silver part aside, but the damage was already done. The black burns where the silver met his skin was proof enough that he wasn't human.

Travis launched at him, digging the broken wood into Lucas's shoulder. Lucas bellowed and pushed him backwards, putting enough distance between the two of them for me to step in.

I turned my back on Lucas, and faced Travis with my hands out. "He tried to help Gram," I said. "He kept her safe until I found her."

"Bull! Why the hell is he still breathing? You took a damn oath when you were sworn into the Guard, Red. Your only purpose is to kill those things!" He pointed at Lucas.

"No. My oath is to protect the people of Dakota from harm. To take down our enemies, and to preserve our way of life. It isn't to kill just because someone is different."

"I bet he is the reason your grandmother is dead," he snarled.

"He's the reason she made it back to this town alive," I countered.

"Traitor. You're just as damned as he is," he snapped and closed his fist around the hilt of his silver blade.

"You're the tracker. Go see for yourself. You know how to read the land. If you see something other than what Gram told me, then by all means, I will do my job," I said. "But my job is not to kill an innocent man who tried to help a hurt woman just because of his heritage. He protected her from the more savage beasts that would have torn her to pieces." I took a breath and lowered my arms. "My job is not to commit an act of murder."

His gaze hardened and fixed on me.

The blade shot out of its sheath, and hot fire engulfed my forearm. I pulled my arm to my body and stared down at the tear in the fabric.

"Did you just cut me?" I yelled as blood discolored my sleeve.

Travis stared at my bloody arm and pressed his lips together. A mixture of disgust and fury filled his face and he turned, marching right out of the house without another word.

"Damn it." I crossed into the bathroom and rolled back the sleeve. The cut was deep, but not deep enough to have hit any major veins. I pulled out the gauze from the cabinet along with some disinfectant. Before I attempted to patch myself up, Lucas took the bottle from my hand.

"It's the least I can do for you," he said quietly and poured some liquid over my cut.

I drew a sharp inhale through my teeth, but didn't make any other noise at the sting sizzling over my wound. He dabbed a cloth to dry the area and then wrapped my forearm in gauze until the damage was covered enough for the blood to be a light pink through the layers. It was a good war wound patch. I glanced up at him after he stowed the disinfectant and gauze away in the cabinet.

“What about yours?” I nodded to the singed tears in his shirt.

“I’m fine,” he said and gave me a crooked smile.

“I think I’ll be the judge of that,” I said.

Lucas rolled his eyes and pulled his sleeve back. The black welt on his arm was nothing like the cut I had. It looked as if he had been branded instead of sliced, and there was no blood to clean up. I reached out and ran my fingers over the rough patch. He pulled his arm away with a grimace.

“What about your shoulder?” His shirt showed red patches where he had pulled out the wooden shaft Travis had stabbed him with.

Lucas pulled the shirt aside so I could see the perfect skin of his shoulder. I lifted my eyebrows.

“We heal pretty quickly when we are hurt with something other than silver.”

“Oh.” My gaze dropped to the blackened marks on his arm. “Gram has an aloe plant in her bedroom. It might help.”

He cocked his head.

"It's for burns."

"I've never heard of it," he said.

I took him by the elbow and led him into Gram's room. On the top of the bookshelf sat a green plant with thick tapered stems sat. I stopped in front of it and pushed his sleeve away from the burns. Reaching up, I grabbed a stem and snapped it. Clear salve oozed from the broken limb, and I quickly drew it across the burn, covering it in the clear goop.

"That actually feels... pleasant," he said, his voice carrying a surprised lilt. He reached beyond me and broke another piece off, covering another welt. When he reached again, I stopped him.

"There is plenty in the piece you have. Just squeeze from the tip, and more aloe will come out."

He did as I instructed, and a smile formed. He looked like a child who had discovered a golden pebble in the brook. It was the kind of smile that made me forget my sorrow.

I glanced around the room, and reality settled in. Travis was mad enough to do something rash like mouth off to the Guard, and if he did that, my life was over. I wasn't going to be able to honor Gram's wishes as far as a funeral was concerned, but I could follow through on her last request. I could make sure nothing else happened to Lucas.

I glanced up at him, and an urgency gripped me. How long had it been since Travis stormed out? Damn it. I turned and left Gram's room. My heart squeezed against the thought of leaving everything I knew, but I had to if I was going to live to see another full moon.

I diverted my focus away from the crippling loss and onto the things that truly mattered to me. If I could just lasso the cottage and drag it with me, this would be so much easier. I hoisted the bow and quiver over my shoulders and grabbed the cookie jar off the counter in the kitchen. In my room, I tossed what little clothing I had into a knapsack along with the cookies.

I glanced at Lucas standing in the doorway, watching me with a perplexed ridge between his eyes.

"We have to leave. Now," I said and grabbed the last item that meant more to me than everything in my backpack combined. The comforter my grandmother quilted for me.

When I turned back to the door, Lucas stood holding the potted aloe plant and wearing a sheepish smile along with his saddlebag slung over his shoulder.

It was my turn to roll my eyes. However, it was a useful plant to have around, so I didn't give him any grief. With my pack full and the blanket slung over my shoulder, I headed for the back door and an unknown future as a fugitive.

Chapter 10

I MADE IT THREE steps into the open when every last one of the guardsmen stepped to the fence with their bows drawn.

My heart leapt into my throat. I didn't dare turn to see if Lucas was behind me or not. If he had stepped out of the house, he was just as exposed as I was.

"Please don't shoot him. He tried to save Gram," I said, lifting my hands so they could see I wasn't armed.

"I don't care. He needs to be put down." Remy's growl came from my right.

I turned, taking a step back so I was closer to Lucas, along with providing us a little protection from the arrows by using the wall to the bathroom as a buffer for our backs.

I knew these men. They were trained to kill werewolves without hesitation. The only reason Lucas was still standing was because I was blocking his front and the house blocked his back.

"Gram asked me to keep him safe," I argued. "It's what she wanted!"

"Move, Red." Remy stared down the shaft of his arrow, lining up the shot.

"Have I ever lied to you?" I glared at Remy and then glanced around at the rest of the Guard, until my gaze landed on Travis standing next to Remy. "To any of you?"

"He has you under some sort of spell," Travis said. "One where you'll say anything to keep him alive."

I took a breath because I needed to weigh the words that parked at the tip of my tongue.

Another life besides ours was in the balance, but if I didn't offer an objective viewpoint, one that would collaborate with what I was saying, there was no way Lucas would make it out of this corral alive. If I moved, Lucas was dead. If I didn't, I had no idea what the Guard would do, especially if they truly thought I was compromised.

"If you don't believe me, ask Doc Wilton. He was there. He heard Gram tell me to make sure nothing happened to Lucas."

Remy's arrow wavered, and he stood taller, measuring my words.

"The doc knew about him?" He pointed his chin towards us.

"Yes." I said. "Besides, when the hell have you ever seen a wolf put a spell on a human?"

"When a human has been bitten." Remy's eyes narrowed in Lucas's direction.

"I have not been bitten," I spat out the words like bitter medicine.

"Prove it," he replied.

The hair on the back of my neck bristled, and I balked at the head of the Guard. I had seen Remy do this before. When one of the guards came back from a hunt alone. I knew what command was coming, and I wasn't in a complying mood.

"How would you like me to prove my innocence?" The growl in my voice was evident. I was sure my glare matched the warning.

The corner of Remy's mouth twitched into a smirk. "Strip."

"I will do no such thing!"

Remy's arrow returned to the taut bow. "Last chance."

I pressed my lips together as heat flared in my face. The last thing I wanted to do was remove my clothing in front of the Guard, but that was the only way we would be able to walk out of here. I handed the blanket tossed over my shoulders to Lucas. Unfortunately, that uncovered the bow and arrows slung over my arm.

"Drop your bow slowly," Remy warned, his face as tense as his bow.

I clenched my hands into fists and closed my eyes, pushing the aggravation crawling over my skin away. I held my hands out to the sides with my fingers splayed as I lowered my shoulder. The bow and quiver slid down to my elbow, and I straightened my arm, letting it drop to the ground.

Remy's bow relaxed, and his hard gaze met mine. He knew I could have taken out a handful of guardsmen before any of them got a shot off, and I thought maybe that action alone would let us off the hook.

"Strip," Remy said when I didn't move.

Grinding my teeth together so I didn't tell him exactly what I thought of his order, I slid my boots off and then my socks, showing him the top and underside of each foot before I continued. My knickers came next, and I slowly turned so everyone could see that I had no bite marks on my lower legs. I hesitated at peeling off my drawers, debating on whether it was better to take off my top first. I was hoping Remy would back off, but I knew better.

The heat in my face spread into my neck and chest, and my fingers fumbled with the buttons on my shirt.

"Is this truly necessary?" Lucas said from behind me.

"Yes," I said at the same time as Remy and some of the other guardsmen. I glanced back at Lucas. "As mortifying as this is, it is necessary. So just shut up," I snapped.

I got to the last button and closed my eyes as I dropped the shirt to the ground, exposing my bare chest. I fought the instinct to cover my breasts and kept my hands busy by dropping my drawers. I stepped out of the fabric towards Remy, put my arms out perpendicular to the ground, and did the slow turn so he could see all my exposed skin.

"Lift your braid," Remy said.

I did as he asked. When I completed my revolution, I lowered my arms and waited for the next set of instructions.

"Get dressed," Remy growled.

I did but I remained blocking Lucas just in case anyone decided to take matters into their own hands and kill the wolf. Once I was fully clothed, I glanced at Remy. A chill rolled across my skin, manifesting my shock. Remy's bow and arrow weren't at the ready. In fact, they were by his side. Only a couple arrows were pointing in our direction. I missed something significant.

When he stepped into the corral, Remy held his hand out. Travis placed silver shackles into his palm, and Remy approached me with an unreadable expression.

"You were always good at those potato sack races," he said and offered me the shackles. "Wrists and ankles."

"Really?" I snatched the silver from his hands and held it up between us. "You could have just handed me this." I shook it for good measure, again proving to the Guard that I hadn't been bitten.

One side of his lips curved and he shrugged. "You betrayed the Guard. I think a long look at the goods was warranted." The hint of humor faded at the low growl that came from behind me. "Cuff him, Red. One on each of you."

"No," I said and shoved the shackles back at him. I saw what silver did to Lucas. I wasn't going to do that to him.

"Then he dies." Both Remy's tone and his hard stare told me he meant business.

"It's okay, Ruby," Lucas said from behind me. "It won't kill me."

I glanced over my shoulder. "That's not the point," I said and turned back to Remy. "He isn't a criminal."

"But he is a werewolf," he said. "And do I have to remind you of how many laws *you've* broken? Put those things on now."

I gritted my teeth. "I'll do it on one condition."

"You have no bartering power here, little girl," Remy said.

"Honor Gram's wishes." I stared him down.

"Do you see me trying to kill him at the moment?" He waved towards Lucas.

"I'm talking about Gram's final resting wishes. You of all people should know what she wanted."

He blinked and took a small step backwards. "We are burying her," he said like that was the only choice.

I shook my head. "That's not what she wanted."

"She still talked about being turned to dust?" he asked.

"Yes. It's called cremation, and that's what she wanted," I said. "I'll shackle us together if you promise me that you will make sure Gram's wishes are honored."

His lips pressed together, and he glared at me. "Put the cuffs on."

I stood taller. "Promise me," I said with the same feral intensity.

He stepped close enough for me to smell the faded scent of cigar on his clothing, and he grabbed the shackles from my hand. After slapping one on my wrist, he snapped the other cuff around Lucas's.

Lucas hissed in pain as the silver burned his skin. Remy crouched down and clasped my right ankle and Lucas's left ankle together. At least the ankle shackle had the fabric of his pants as a buffer. When Remy stood, he grabbed the chain between our wrists and yanked us forward.

"Depending upon what the judge renders, you may be in the plot next to your grandmother," he snarled as he marched us out of the corral.

Chapter 11

THE MOON SHONE THROUGH the window of the cell I sat in. Lucas was still tethered to the silver cuff, and his harried breathing and occasional stifled groans echoed in the dark chamber of the jail. The binds holding him also prohibited him from shifting, and based on the sounds he made, it must have hurt something fierce.

Remy had left us here so he could attend my grandmother's funeral. The entire town would pay their respects, but I wasn't allowed to be there for either the service or the gathering that always followed a funeral here in Dakota. My heart ached. I wouldn't be able to say a proper goodbye.

I wondered if Remy would honor Gram's wishes. I wondered what the town would do to me, and I feared what they would do to Lucas.

I glanced through the bars at him and sighed. As if sensing my gaze, he looked up, his bright blue eyes glowing in the dim light of the moon.

"I'm sorry. I should have left last night," he said in a weak voice.

"This isn't your fault. I asked you to stay," I said. If I had let him go, neither of us would be rotting in jail waiting for our trial.

He closed his eyes and turned away from me. "I should have known better."

He leaned his head against the adjoining bars close enough for me to touch him. His thick hair beckoned me, and I reached out, running my fingers through the lush strands. Lucas jerked away and glanced over his shoulder. A crease formed between his eyes.

"What are you doing?"

"I, um. I just. I don't know." I stumbled on the words, wondering the same thing. His hair was just so... touchable. I shook my head and clasped my hands in my lap. I had no idea what the hell had come over me.

He slowly turned back around with a sigh. "Why didn't you kill me?"

I remained quiet, and when he glanced back, I just raised my eyebrows.

"You grandmother," he said with a disappointed lilt. He relaxed into the bars again and let out a soft laugh. "She wasn't the least bit afraid when I approached her. She got a bit ornery, though, especially when she thought I was in league with the other wolf and toying with her." He sighed. "She was quite a lady," he added after a few minutes of silence.

"Yes, she was." I lay back on the thin mattress, distancing myself from the need to run my fingers through his thick hair, and ignored the lump that formed in my throat and the sting in my eyes.

"You're a lot like her, you know," Lucas said.

I wasn't anything like my grandmother. She had been so strong and so independent and so loved by the townspeople.

Lucas turned towards the hall just as a shuffle reached my ears.

"Why?" A gruff voice said from the shadows.

Travis stepped into the light, his eyes rimmed red and his cheeks flushed. He reeked of alcohol, even from this distance. Just the fact he was here after dark said volumes as to his state of mind.

"Why what?"

"Why did you allow that thing in your house? In your bedroom?"

"First of all, *that thing* has a name. And secondly, he saved Gram from dying alone."

"Then you say thank you, and go on your way. You don't invite the enemy into your bed!"

"Go home, Travis. You are drunk," I said. I wasn't going to have this conversation with him, especially with Lucas in the adjoining cell.

"I did not sleep with Ruby," Lucas said.

My heart twisted. I didn't need Lucas's help with this argument. It would only make things worse.

"I'm not talking to you, so shut up," Travis growled through the bars, his glare murderous.

Lucas raised his untethered hand in a sign of withdrawal from the conversation and stretched out on his cot as best he could with his wrist and ankle shackled to the bed. “You know what? You’re right. I should have left after she came home devastated from her grandmother’s death. I should have left her alone to deal with her grief and just thought of myself.”

“Shut up,” Travis yelled.

“You’re not helping,” I said to Lucas.

“I see the way you look at him,” Travis said. “He has you under some sort of spell.”

I stared at Travis and took a deep breath. “How long have we known each other?”

“Too long,” he muttered under his breath.

“Have I ever lied to you?”

He shuffled outside the bars and kicked the dirt. “No.”

“Then why don’t you believe me?”

“Because the girl I know wouldn’t have let a werewolf live.”

He had a point. Prior to the encounter with my grandmother, I would have put an arrow between the wolf’s eyes without question, but it was my grandmother's plea that kept me from killing Lucas.

"What if they are not all bad? What if there are some good ones out there? Ones that don't kill humans?"

Travis stepped back into the shadows.

"What if all our assumptions are wrong?" The fact that I voiced the core issue eating at me since I stowed my bow and arrow away that night was a step in the right direction. But it was also one that made me question my job, my duty to kill without thought, and made me wonder who the actual monsters were.

"They killed your parents, Red. They kill. That's what they are created for. To kill." His words had enough venom to tingle across my skin.

"That's what we are trained to do, too." I couldn't stop the words from tumbling out. "We were trained to think they are evil creatures. That their only purpose is to kill humans." I got to my feet and crossed to where he stood. "We were taught to be just as much of a monster as they are."

Travis glared at me through the bars.

"We were taught wrong," I added softly.

"No. You weren't," Lucas said, and I spun towards his cage. "Not entirely. Most werewolves don't know how to control their primal urges. A wolf in the wild hunts for food. They don't discern between humans and animals in that facet. A human turned werewolf is a different story. The venom does something to their minds almost in the same way rabies turns a docile dog into a monster."

Travis's gaze narrowed.

"Very few can contain the need to destroy. At least that's what I've found in my limited travels," Lucas added.

"So why should I believe you are any different?" Travis asked without much hostility.

Lucas sat up. "If I was one of those things," he started with a voice filled with disdain, "Ruby and her grandmother would have died on the floor of that ravine."

I stared at him and then turned back to Travis. "I know you don't believe him, or me for that matter. But you are the best tracker in this region. Go find the truth yourself. It's all out there, at the base of that ravine."

His lips pressed together and he shook his head. "Do you understand what is going to happen to you? No one in this town will believe your story. No one," he whispered, and his eyes filled up with tears. He reached for me through the bars.

I stepped out of his range. “Then you better go find the truth for yourself.”

He stared at me and gave a slow nod before turning and disappearing into the shadows. I walked to the cot and lay down again, staring at the ceiling as I processed the conversation.

“Are you okay?” Lucas said after a while.

“So, all converted werewolves are monsters?” I glanced over at him.

“Not all, but most. Especially if they have an alpha that thrives on chaos and murder. It goes without saying that the pack will follow suit.”

I chewed on a hangnail and studied the ceiling. “And if they don’t?”

“They are usually exiled or killed if they don’t comply.” Bitterness crept into his voice. “That’s what happened to my father. He still had all his faculties and did not wish to harm humans. If he had, I would have never been born.”

“Are there others like your father?”

“I don’t know,” he said softly and met my gaze. “I don’t even know if there are any like me out there. I’m the only one in these parts, at least that’s the impression I’ve gotten, but who knows. Somewhere, there could be a community where humans and werewolves live in harmony, but I have yet to hear of such a thing."

"Farmer and dreamer," I said.

He gave me a soft smile and a shrug. His eyes still held deep pain, but at least he had gotten control over his audible reaction to the silver.

Then his smile faded. "What will happen to you?"

I huffed a laugh and returned my gaze to the ceiling. "If the town finds me guilty, I'll be put in front of an archery squad before nightfall."

Lucas's eyes slowly widened.

"Just because they loved my grandmother, doesn't mean they will spare me from a traitor's fate."

"Traitor?" His voice cracked.

"Yes. Violating curfew comes with jail time. But allowing a werewolf to live..." I shrugged. "That comes with a death sentence."

"That is just as barbaric as pack mentality," he said.

The silence between us was stifling, but I wasn't going to disagree with him.

“Have you ever...” He turned away before he finished asking the question, like he didn’t want to know the answer.

“Have I ever been on the firing line?” I finished it for him, and when he wouldn’t look at me, I sighed. “No. I wasn’t old enough to be in the firing line. But I was old enough to bear witness. It haunts me to this day.” I looked out at the moon. “I question just about everything, which has put me in hot water more than a time or two, but I’ve never questioned the purpose of the Guard. We are here to keep Dakota safe. For the record, I still agree with that purpose. It’s a noble pursuit, but I don’t always agree with the manner in which we follow through on it. We can act without mercy.” I shrugged. “We can be barbaric.”

He nodded slowly.

“But the wolves we have put down operate under the same umbrella. Without mercy. Without regard to age. Without exception. So mercy has never been warranted.” I closed my eyes. “Until you wandered into that ravine, mercy wasn’t a thing I ever entertained before. I never thought I could actually carry on a conversation with a wolf, never mind find myself...” I bit my tongue. There was no use telling him I was attracted to him in a way I had never experienced.

He sat up and turned towards me. When he reached through the bars and took my hand in his, my heart started a skipping beat that encompassed my entire chest. His touch was gentle and his fingers smooth, much like his chest had felt under my hand. The skin-to-skin contact dulled my mind and turned my body into a raging inferno of heat. I pulled from his grip, but a small smile toyed on his lips and he glanced at the bars separating us.

He opened his mouth and then closed it. “Please finish what you were going to say,” he finally said as his gaze locked on mine.

“Locked in a cell because of a wolf,” I said, avoiding the truth biting every inch of my skin.

His eyes narrowed and then he lay down on the mattress and closed his eyes, dousing the blue glow lighting the small space. An uncomfortable silence blanketed the cells, and all I could think about was how disappointed my grandmother would have been.

Chapter 12

A RUCKUS IN THE hallway pulled me out of the doze I had fallen into. I sat up to see the constable shoving a very intoxicated version of Remy into the adjoining cell. Belligerent was an understatement as the head of the Guard spewed slurred vulgarities.

“What happened?” I asked as Remy fell onto the mattress and immediately began snoring.

Constable Murphy looked at me and turned to leave.

“What did Remy do?” I asked again before he disappeared.

“He desecrated a grave,” the constable said over his shoulder. “And had a bonfire in his backyard.”

Remy’s fingers were covered in dirt, and soot streaked his cheeks. He must have followed through on Gram’s wishes despite the consequences. I could no longer contain the grief bubbling just below the surface. My throat tightened and I stretched out on the bed, letting tears escape the corners of my eyes.

Lucas’s fingers clasped mine. His tired blue eyes shined in the dim light as he gave my hand a squeeze.

Tears flowed and my breath hitched. In the morning light, the reality of our situation settled into every fiber of my body, and with it came an ungodly fear.

I didn’t want to die, and I certainly didn’t want Lucas to be killed. I wanted to explore whatever had sparked between us, but it was a useless dream. A luxury we would have to forgo because I was fool enough to have asked him to stay.

“I’m sorry,” Lucas whispered.

I wiped my face with my free hand and glanced at him through the bars. I couldn't find the words to tell him this was my fault, that the death he waited for with such grace was my doing. I should have killed him on the spot, it would have been more humane. Instead, I shook my head and stared back at the ceiling through blurred vision.

The cell brightened as the morning progressed, and my dread manifested in uncontrollable bouts of shivers despite the warmth bathing the cell. It wouldn't be long before we were paraded through the town to stand in front of the court. Deep in my bones, I knew it was only for show. The sentence wouldn't alter from those before me. A selfish part of me hoped I would face the firing line first so I wouldn't have to witness Lucas's death, but I knew better. They would want me to reflect on my mistakes before they ended my life. They wanted me to taste the bitterness of my choices.

I closed my eyes and shuddered. Mercy wasn't in Dakota's vocabulary where werewolves were concerned. And I couldn't blame them. I carried that exact mindset the day I went out with Remy and Travis. But that mindset changed sometime during the night in Lucas's house with Gram.

Silence blanketed the cells, and then Remy's scruffy voice filled the space.

"Red?"

I looked over at him, and his bloodshot gaze met mine.

"Why didn't you tell me?" he whispered.

"Tell you what?"

He reached into his pocket and dropped a folded piece of paper through the bars. I crossed and picked it up, unfolding it in the light. Gram's neat handwriting scrawled across the paper. I stared at the words and stepped backwards, dropping the note, like distancing myself would change what Gram had told Remy.

I stared at the paper as it fluttered to the floor and then locked my gaze with Remy.

He chuckled. "I gather from your reaction you didn't know either."

My high-pitched laugh confirmed his assessment.

"It actually explains why you're the best shot I've ever seen, but still, finding out you're my blood just as you're facing the firing line?" He rubbed his face and glanced away. "Your grandmother had a sick sense of humor."

He swung his legs over the side of the cot and groaned. I turned to Lucas, and his blue eyes sent a shiver through me, adding to the clanging of my heart and the pounding in my temples. My mouth went dry.

Before I had a chance to truly digest the confession laid out in the note, the constable came down the stairs with a dozen guards, none of which I had ever partnered with on any of our wolf runs.

Four of them waited at my door while the constable unlocked the cell, and the other eight waited outside Lucas's cell with their silver daggers drawn. The hatred in their expressions tightened the muscles of my throat.

"Don't hurt him," I said with as much force in my voice as I could muster.

The only one that acknowledged my order was Seth, one of the older guards, but the look he gave me didn't settle my nerves. His smile promised pain.

Lucas got to his feet and braced himself, taking the links of the chain between the silver wristband and the bars. The muscles in his jaw tightened and the stench of burning flesh wafted through the cell.

"No!" I shouted.

Four guards grabbed hold of my arms, dragging me out of the cell. Lucas's door was thrown wide, and the guards filtered in.

"Remy, do something!" I screamed, then the door at the bottom of the stairs cut off my view of the attack on Lucas.

I stopped fighting my captors and let them lead me to the town square. I scanned the crowd. The entire town came out for this trial. Outside of Remy and the guards taking justice into their own hands in Lucas's cell, there was only one person missing. I scanned again to make sure.

Travis wasn't there.

Tears burned my eyes, but I blinked them back. I refused to cry in front of this ungrateful town. Anger finally burned through all the emotions accosting me. My skin heated from it, but I straightened my spine in defiance.

Judge Murphy cleared his throat and looked at the paper in front of him before looking up at me like he had swallowed a bug. Disgust formed in the lines around his mouth, and I glared at him.

"Ruby Locklear, you have been found guilty of high treason." He nodded at the guards holding me.

This wasn't like any of the other court proceedings I had witnessed. "I don't get to say anything in my defense?" I yelled out over the crowd.

"Did you allow that wolf to live?" he snarled at me.

"Yes, but he..."

“Silence!” He stood and pointed towards the post in the center of the courtyard.

“I will not be silent. If trying to save my grandmother is considered a crime, then we are guilty.” I scanned the crowd as the guards dragged me to one of two posts and strapped my arms around the back. “The wolf saved her. Killing him would have been murder for the sake of bloodlust, just like the monsters out there!” I nodded towards the northern woods.

A murmur blanketed the bystanders, and some shifted their weight, glancing at their neighbors before looking at the ground.

“Gram said she fell, and that wolf who is being brutalized right now kept her warm and protected her from another wolf attack!”

Judge Murphy glanced at the guards. “Silence her,” he ordered.

One turned and shoved a handkerchief into my mouth, muffling my argument. I struggled against the binds, and my gaze jumped from face to face until it landed on Doc Wilton. The moment we made eye contact, he looked away.

I needed him to speak up.

A commotion from the jail erupted. The crowd parted as the guards dragged a beaten and bruised Lucas to the post next to me. He didn’t even get the pretense of a trial. They just strung his half conscious body up by his wrists. He sagged from the binds, and his head lolled to the side.

I shook my head, trying to spit out the fabric in my mouth.

The Guard took their places in the firing line.

Finally, I coughed out the rag. “Please, Doc. Please tell them he didn’t hurt Gram!” I cried.

Silence settled as all eyes turned toward the town doctor.

He shifted his weight and stared at the ground before he finally looked up and nodded. “The wolf displayed kindness and civility, and Gram Locklear requested my silence under doctor-patient confidentiality. She confirmed what Red said earlier. He provided her warmth, shelter, and protection when he could have easily ripped her to shreds.”

“See?” I said.

“The law states you both must die.” Judge Murphy held up the town law book.

The sound of hoofs hitting dirt pulled our attention away, and Travis rode in on Midnight, stopping the horse between us and the firing line. Both my horse and Travis were out of breath.

"Move, boy," Judge Murphy said.

"I have some information that may sway judgment," Travis said from his perch on the horse. He turned to the Guard lined up with their silver arrows. "He isn't normal." He nodded towards Lucas. "He may be a werewolf, but I'll be goddamned if Red wasn't telling the truth. He has a healthy farm filled with healthy living animals. He has a garden. And it looks like the only thing stored in his icebox is venison."

"He is a wolf," the judge emphasized.

Travis shrugged. "I haven't seen him turn. Have you?"

"But his eyes," Seth said from the firing line beyond Travis.

"You all know what kind of tracking skills I have," Travis said and glanced at me. "Red reminded me of that last night, so I went at first light and tracked down what happened. There was no sign of foul play in the orchard. Gram fell. But the patterns along with the dead wolf at the base of the hill confirm Red's version of the story. So does the farm and the conversation I had with Doc Wilton after Gram's funeral yesterday. Hell, the wolf is more of a gentleman than any of us." He glanced at the Guard. "Not one of us averted our eyes when she stripped down to show she hadn't been bitten. None of us looked away. But the wolf didn't look at her."

“Maybe he just isn’t interested,” Seth said with his bow at the ready, likely waiting for Travis to move Midnight out of his line of sight.

Travis sucked air in through his lips. “He’s interested. I’ve seen the way he looks at her when she isn’t looking, and believe me, it’s a look that can’t be mistaken. But when she undressed, he did not look. He stared out at his mare, at the sky, at us. But not at her.” His cheeks reddened. “And be honest. None of us were inspecting her for wolf bites.”

Faces reddened enough to rival my hair. Heat filled my own cheeks, and I glanced at Lucas. His gaze met mine.

“I couldn’t stop staring at her until I noticed his behavior, and then all I felt was shame. Shame because I knew what I was doing wasn’t for the good of this town. It was purely selfish. But this...this...” Travis looked back at Lucas. “This beast showed more restraint than any of us.”

“Wolves don’t show restraint no matter what form they take,” I said. “And they certainly don’t raise chickens, or cattle, or have a mare that would walk through fire for him.”

“Are you a werewolf?” the judge asked Lucas.

“If you’re asking if I’m one of those heinous beasts out there attacking the innocent? No. But if you're asking if I shift into wolf form when the sun sets? The answer to that is yes."

"You don't shift at will?"

My head turned at Remy's gruff voice. He stood in front of the judge's chair waiting for his own sentence to be rendered.

"No. My change is subjected to the rise and setting of the sun."

"Lucas is different," I stressed. "He had so many opportunities to kill both Gram and me, but he didn't. That has to mean something?"

"He is a wolf. There are laws."

"Yes, there are laws, but isn't there also mercy? Are we to persecute him just because he was born into this life? It was not a choice for him, just like it wasn't a choice for me to have red hair. It was part of my heritage. Are we that cruel and heinous? Are we more like the pack we hunt or more like the humans we serve to protect?"

My words didn't appear to sway the mob, so I turned my appeal to my grandfather and the Guard.

"I have had your back all these years." I moved my gaze to each of them. "I still do. And out of everyone in this town, you know me best. You know the hell I endured, the pain I suppressed and tapped every time I went on a hunt. You know mercy isn't a part of my makeup."

I turned my gaze to Remy. "The oath we took to protect Dakota is to protect life. This, what you are doing now, this is taking life for no other reason than fear of the unknown. If you do this, you will be no better than the cold-blooded killers we hunt."

Travis turned toward Lucas. "Have you ever killed a human?"

"No." Lucas's answer blanketed the crowd.

Travis glanced at the judge and shrugged his good arm.

Before the judge could speak, I asked Lucas, "Have you ever killed a werewolf?"

"Yes. I slaughtered the pack that killed my parents, and I have been on my own ever since."

A hush fell on the square.

"I've got a bounty on my head just like Ruby does."

Both Travis's and Remy's gazes snapped towards Lucas.

"Red has a bounty on her?" they asked in unison.

I glanced at Lucas. He just gave them a reason to kill him, but apparently that hadn't crossed his mind before he blew the one chance we had of getting out of here alive.

"So, you figured what? You'd snatch Red and get back into the good graces of the pack?" Judge Murphy asked. "Pull the wool over her eyes and get her thinking you are not like the rest of those beasts out there?"

Lucas blinked and shook his head. "No. I didn't even know who she was until she led me and my horse into her grandmother's corral." He shivered. "Those wolves draped over her fence posts were kind of a dead giveaway." A twitch of a smile formed on his lips. "Pun intended."

Remy chuckled and so did Travis. Travis's gaze met mine from on top of my horse. He offered me his best "I tried" smile, and I acknowledged it with a nod.

"My mother was human. I want nothing to do with a pack that has its sights on killing people," Lucas added. "And from what I've been able to gather, the pack that's here now wants to wipe out this settlement."

"How would you know that?" I asked.

Lucas huffed. "The wolf who was going to kill your grandmother gave me an ultimatum. Join the pack and slaughter the citizens of Dakota, or die with them. Since you are still breathing, you can figure out the choice I made." He glanced out at the crowd. "When I chased him away, he said I better enjoy the next few days because on the night of the full moon, rivers of blood will flow through this town."

A panicked murmur started amongst the townspeople, and they huddled closer together. Tonight was the full moon.

"So, you go ahead. You kill your only shot at taking out this pack," he added as the whispers rose. "Without Ruby, you do not have a prayer."

"And without Lucas, you do not have me," I said, leveraging the gauntlet Lucas so brilliantly wielded.

The entire town fell silent for five beats of my heart.

"How many of them are there?" Remy asked.

Lucas looked past me at my newly revealed grandfather. "I don't know. So far, I've caught somewhere between five and six dozen unique scent signatures, but I can't be sure. Those wolf carcasses around her corral messed up my sense of smell, and because of the silver cuffs, I wasn't able to shift last night. When I'm in wolf form, everything is much... keener."

"You are saying the pack is sixty wolves at minimum?" Remy asked in a gob-smacked tone I had never heard from him.

"I think it's more in the realm of seventy."

The crowd erupted, and I smelled fear on the air.

How in the hell could seventy werewolves hide from our hunting jaunts? The blood in my veins turned cold. Either these were cunning creatures or Lucas was feeding a load of bull to the crowd. Either way, it was working.

I met Remy's gaze, and he just shook his head slowly, still trying to digest the last couple minutes. The Guard was only comprised of twenty members between the age of ten and seventy. Half of them couldn't hit a still wolf with a brick at two paces, never mind multiple wolves on the attack. We'd even had our losses with groups of three trolling the woods.

Remy turned to the judge. "We need her." His statement was absolute.

The judge's lips compressed together until they were nonexistent. The bloom in his red cheeks burned brighter, and his nostrils flared. His gaze jumped from Remy to mine.

"You have just earned yourself a stay of execution while we discuss this matter. Put them back in a holding cell," he ordered.

I looked up at Travis and mouthed the words 'thank you' as guards unclasped me from the post and led me away.

Chapter 13

LUCAS LAY ON HIS side on the cot facing me as I paced in the same cell. Heated murmurs of the townspeople drifted into the window, and I strained to hear what their arguments were or who was taking each side.

"Ruby?" Lucas's soft voice broke through my concentration.

His eyes had dulled considerably from this morning.

I stopped pacing as my heart went on overdrive. “Are you okay?” I asked, which brought forth a tight smile.

Lucas pushed himself up on the cot with a wince and climbed to his feet. “You shouldn’t have laid your life on the line for me.”

“Are there really that many wolves out there?” I asked.

Lucas gave me a slow nod as he steadied himself on his feet.

“And are you one of them?” I asked, because I couldn’t quite silence the nagging distrust inside me. Despite all he had done, and despite the underlying attraction vibrating through every cell, I still couldn’t quite trust him with my whole heart.

He was still a werewolf.

He shook his head. “No.” He bit his lip and glanced out the window. He crossed the space between us, wincing with every other step until he loomed over me.

I took in his wounds. Besides the ugly black rings around his wrists, his shirt and pants had been slashed in several places. He had over a dozen silver burns based on the holes in his clothes.

"Did they..." I waved at him and gulped. "I can see they cut you, but did they... did they stab you?" The words squeaked out, and the discomfort under my skin increased at the thought of a blade puncturing his skin.

"It doesn't matter."

My gaze jumped up to his. It did matter. It mattered a great deal, and I pressed my lips against letting those words tumble out.

"I can feel the pull of the alpha," he whispered. His hands clenched and unclenched, and his jaw tightened. "He wants this town painted with the blood of the dead. Everyone except for the archer with the fiery hair."

I stepped away. "Why didn't you tell me this?"

"I'm telling you now." His eyes flared bright in the tight space. "I went out that night because I heard the call. The alpha is calling every last werewolf in the region to join him in this massacre." He glanced up at the ceiling and shook his head. "Your grandmother... I don't know how, but she was able to break the spell that bastard had over me."

My heart jumped in my chest, and I stepped back into the wall of bars at the other side of the cell, distancing myself from him.

Lucas locked his gaze on me. “I’d like to believe I wouldn’t have hurt her if that other wolf wasn’t already tormenting her,” he said and his gaze dropped. “What I’m trying to tell you is you should have let them kill me, because the alpha…” He stepped closer. “I don’t know if I can resist his command.”

His hands came up and cupped my chin. Just his touch in such an intimate manner doused my skin with heat so strong I nearly melted into him. His thumb trailed over my bottom lip, and he stared at it before his hungry gaze found mine again.

When he leaned forward and pressed his warm lips against mine, my mind spun with the sweetness of his kiss. When his tongue traced my lips, I opened my mouth, letting our tongues intertwine in a dance so slow and seductive that I forgot we were in a jail cell.

His hands slid lower, molding over my breasts with such a light touch I moaned into his mouth. God help me. Molten lava formed low in my belly, and I gasped at the heat enveloping me. His lips moved to my cheek, to my neck, and I closed my eyes at the silkiness of his touch.

“Lucas.” His name escaped in a sultry whisper that felt like home on my tongue.

“You taste like honey,” he whispered against my neck. His lips followed the line from my shoulder to my ear. He took my earlobe between his teeth, applying pressure.

I squealed at the sensation.

Lucas gasped and stepped away abruptly, his eyes wide and his breathing ragged.

Hurt flared in the center of my chest at his horrified look, and I wrapped my arms around my torso to shield myself.

"I almost bit you." He ran his hand through his hair and took another step back. "I don't know which is worse, having that alpha bastard in my head or having you in my heart."

I swallowed and wished I could flee from this cell. I wished I hadn't felt his hands on my body or his lips on mine because now... now a new fear tingled in my bones. If anything happened to Lucas, I was afraid I'd never feel that all-consuming spark again.

The door creaked above, and six guardsmen came down before either of us could speak. Seth stood outside the cell with an unreadable expression. None of them gave any hint of the verdict.

"The court is ready for you," Seth said and swung the door open.

I crossed and noted neither guard who flanked me took hold of me. But the other guards grabbed Lucas's arms as they led us out of the cell. My heart plummeted. Whether these men realized it or not, their actions clued me in to the judgment.

Lucas wasn't going to be spared, regardless of my ultimatum. I wouldn't defend a town that insisted on murdering an innocent man. Donning my inner rebel, I prepared myself for a different kind of battle.

I positioned myself as close to Lucas as possible without touching him to show the town where my loyalties stood. Remy stepped forward in front of the judge. I glanced at his stoic face and then at the guardsmen who filled in the space around him.

"Red, we need you," he said. "We've been your family since your parents died. And as much as I resented your grandmother for insisting I bring you into the fold, I can't say I ever regretted you fighting alongside us. I think it was your grandmother's way of letting me share a part of your life without giving up her ghosts."

A lump formed in my throat at the mention of my grandmother, and I blinked the stinging mist from my eyes.

"Unfortunately, there are laws that we must abide," he added, and his gaze traveled to Lucas. "We cannot..." He clenched his fists, staring at the ground.

The judge cleared his throat.

"We cannot just let you go," Remy said through clenched teeth. "But we also cannot be the ones to murder you, as Red put it earlier." He waved towards me and pressed his lips together. The disdain etched into his face was usually reserved for my antics, but this time, I got the impression he didn't agree with the sentence about to be delivered.

"If he is wanted by the werewolves, we will leave him to their justice." He nodded towards the poles, and the guard dragged him to stand between the two posts.

They clasped one wrist in a silver cuff that hung from one post and then took off the shackles before securing his other wrist. The positioning gave him minimal leeway.

"He's as good as dead shackled like that," I said, appalled.

"He has a chance. If he survives the night, we will let him go," Remy said.

"What if none of us survive?" I asked.

"Then he dies of starvation, instead."

Lucas lifted his nose like he was trying to catch a scent. He glanced over his shoulder at me, his eyes full of regret, but it was nothing compared to the hurt racking my insides. I'd asked him to stay. He would have left if I hadn't uttered that fateful plea.

"No." I turned back towards Remy.

"We are going to hide the entire town in the church, and the Guard will set up a perimeter so nothing gets through."

"I told you, if Lucas isn't spared, I'm not fighting."

Remy's face reddened. "We aren't putting a dozen arrows into his chest," he growled. "He is being spared from our justice."

I swallowed and dropped my gaze to the ground, understanding the mentality of the town. They saw this as mercy, and I knew this was the best they were going to offer, but I didn't have to like it. I finally gave a nod.

"Then my perimeter is between Lucas and the woods." I could stop whatever came out of those woods as long as I was armed with enough arrows.

"We wanted you guarding the doors to the church," the judge said from behind Remy.

I glanced over my shoulder at the church, which stood a little farther than fifty yards from where Lucas was strung up. "If I'm set up at the steps of the church, Lucas will block my line of sight. So will these damn posts. If you want to doom the entire town, be my guest." If they could play games, so could I.

"Red," Travis whispered, holding Midnight's reins. "Be reasonable."

I let out a laugh. "Reasonable? You want me to be reasonable? You're the one that put me in this position," I snapped, the anger bursting through with a vengeance. "You are asking me to walk away from the man who tried to save my grandmother. Does that sound reasonable to you?"

I glared at the crowd and then met Remy's gaze. "As long as Lucas is here within the town limits, we have as much of an obligation to protect him as we have to protect every man, woman, and child that lives here. My perimeter is right here." I walked ten paces in front of Lucas and dug my heel into the ground, creating an arc in the dirt. I stepped to the center of my line and glanced out at the woods again. I had enough space between the trees and where I would be crouched to take on whatever those woods dished out.

"You need to listen to them," Lucas said, pulling my defiant gaze away from the woods. "If you are this close to the woods..." He shook his head.

My lips turned up at the corners. Lucas may have heard the rumors about me, but he really only had a cursory look at what I could do with a bow and arrow. He needed to know why I was on a werewolf's most wanted list, and I was going to give him a front row seat to the show.

Remy's gaze traveled over the vantage point I had chosen, and then he glanced back at the church. His bottom lip sucked in between his teeth as he silently considered my plan.

"Red is right. That is the best spot to defend the church," he said to the judge. "Forcing her to defend from right in front of the church will put us at a disadvantage. There are too many blind spots from the steps even without the werewolf chained to the posts."

"How many arrows do we have?" I asked.

"We only have forty silver-tipped arrows left."

Goosebumps broke out over my arms and I spun, staring at Remy. If Lucas's numbers were right, and we all hit our marks, that still left at minimum twenty wolves that we would have to kill with our daggers. Even one-on-one, that was a stretch, but four-on-one, that was suicide.

My heart thundered in my chest, and my gaze jumped to Lucas and the shackles holding him in place. We had silver, but it wasn't in the right form to kill a werewolf.

"Do we have time to melt down the remaining silver and coat the regular arrows?" I asked as I looked to the sky.

Remy turned towards the judge. “We need more arrows in order to win this battle. No one has had a chance to make a silver run in the last few weeks, and right now, the only silver left is the shackles we took off the prisoner and the ones holding him to the pole. We need it, otherwise...”

“We cannot let the werewolf go,” the judge said.

“Then lock him up in the jail, and we can figure this out tomorrow,” Remy said. “Because without that silver... There. Will. Be. No. Tomorrow.”

I had heard Remy aggravated and forceful, but it did not compare to the doom he painted with those five words.

When the judge didn’t respond, he added, “And we are not using one of the arrows we currently have on him. We need double what we have, and I’m not sacrificing this entire town on this single wolf, especially since I don’t agree with the verdict. Lock him up.”

Another shock skipped through my heart, almost jerking me in place. I didn’t think I’d ever hear Remy Steele stand up for a werewolf, and from the open-mouthed expression of most of the crowd, I thought they were all in the same place I was. We were witnessing a miracle.

I glanced out at the woods. I just hoped it wasn't the only miracle today.

Chapter 14

I STOOD WITH JOHN, the blacksmith, as he melted down the chains. He hunched over the extreme heat, painstakingly turning the bowl of silver until it was liquid. I handed him each arrow, and he dunked the tip. We had enough to coat twenty more arrows, which left a whole bunch of ifs.

John wasn't much of a talker, so he wandered around the shop, doing what I imagine he usually did during a normal day. When he thought the arrows were dry enough, he put them in my quiver.

"You really think you can save this town?" he asked.

I glanced at our meager bounty and sighed. "You might want to start praying now," I said and slung the quiver over my shoulder.

"Are you any good with a sword?" he asked after I turned to leave.

I had some instruction, but I wasn't as good as Travis. "Is it made of silver?" If it wasn't, it wouldn't help a lick.

"The finest. It's the strongest steel coated with pure Alberta silver." He reached behind one of the counters and pulled out a long thin sheath with a thick black handle sticking out. He offered it to me. "For when you run out of arrows."

"Thank you, John," I said and took the sword, pulling the blade out far enough to inspect the fine craftsmanship. The blade had intricate designs carved into the silver. "It is beautiful." I tested the blade on the pad of my thumb. "And sharp," I said, offering him a smile of appreciation.

He gave me a nod. "Stay safe, Red."

"Do you have any more silver swords?"

He nodded and stepped towards the back.

"You might need some of those in the church, just in case," I said, stopping him.

He turned and gave me a haunted nod.

"Thank you for this." I held up the sword and left without another word. I had to go give Remy the bad news.

I crossed to the green where Remy was discussing strategy with the other guards and dropped my full quiver at his feet next to the rest of the arrows.

"How many?" he asked.

"Twenty."

A slow whistle came from between his teeth, and he closed his eyes. His shoulders dropped, and my heart plummeted with them. Seeing defeat in Remy's demeanor was more unsettling than the knowledge we didn't have nearly enough firepower.

Remy raked his hand over his face. "We don't even know what direction they'll be coming from."

I chewed my bottom lip and stepped in the direction of where they had Lucas locked up.

“Where do you think you’re going?” he asked.

“I’m going to find out if we can narrow that down,” I said over my shoulder and headed towards the jail. It was worth a shot, especially since he was the one who gave us a heads-up and the head count of the pack.

I glanced at Travis as I crossed to the door separating the constable’s work space with the jail. He wanted to be out with the Guard, even with his arm immobile, but he would probably be the first to be killed out in the open with little to defend himself beyond a broadsword his father gave him. He couldn’t shoot an arrow with one arm. His scowl broadcasted just how unhappy he was with his current assignment—babysitting the werewolf.

I descended the short stairwell and stepped into the dank holding cell, crossing to the bars. Lucas lay with his back to the door. He didn’t budge when I walked in.

“Lucas?” I asked from outside his cell.

He turned slowly, his jaw tightened, and he sat up. He tried to hide the wince, but it didn’t fool me. He pushed up from the cot, crossed slowly to where I stood, and went to wrap his hand around the bar, but pulled it away before he touched the iron.

I reached through the bars and grabbed his hand so I could look at it.

"Don't," he said, his voice scratchy.

I peeled his fingers open and stared at the black marks burned into his skin. Without thinking, I brought his palm to my lips and gently kissed the scar.

"Ruby," he whispered. His voice held a deep longing, one that echoed in my heart. His gaze lingered on my lips before it rose to mine. "Stay with me."

I raised my eyebrows. "We can talk about that tomorrow."

He pulled his hand away. "You cannot fathom what is coming," he snarled and closed his eyes, leaning his head against the bars. "Five of you cannot possibly fight that many werewolves on your own."

"We have no choice. You said they were coming to kill all of us. What would you have us do?"

His head snapped up, and his eyes flared. "Run," he said with no hesitation. "Hide."

"You of all people can't possibly think there is anywhere to hide from those beasts?"

His face scrunched up in pain as he gripped the bars. "You could hide at your grandmother's house. The stench of death makes all animals avoid your property."

“So they wouldn’t come in from that direction?”

Lucas laughed. “No. They will steer clear of that direction.”

“Where will they come from?” I asked softly.

“Every other direction, like a tidal wave. I can feel their presence. I can feel their malice on the air.” He shivered.

“So, the east will be clear, but they will come from the north, south, and west?”

He nodded.

“Where is the greatest concentration?”

Lucas shrugged. “I don’t know.”

I hung my head and took a deep breath, letting it out slowly before I looked back at him. “I will survive this,” I said with a voice much stronger than I felt. I wasn’t sure if it was for his benefit or mine.

He reached out and ran his hands into my hair, pulling me as close as the bars would allow. His bright blue eyes blazed. He ran his thumb across my cheekbone. “That is what I am terrified of.”

I pressed my cheek into his palm, trying to read what was behind those beautiful eyes. "Why?"

"Because I can still feel the alpha trying to weasel his way into my head," he said. "He knows."

"He knows what?"

Lucas's fingers moved to my lips, tracing them tenderly before meeting my gaze. "He doesn't have control over me anymore."

"What changed?"

The corners of his lips tilted into a smile. "I kissed you."

Heat filled my cheeks, and I glanced over his shoulder out the window at the far side of the cell. The memory lingered, and the heat from my cheeks spread through me.

"I wish I could kiss you now," he whispered.

I moved my gaze back to his. I wanted that, too. I wanted more than a kiss. I wanted a lifetime of his kisses. The realization made every muscle in my body ache for him. I stepped away because I needed that type of want in my soul. I needed something to fight for, something to survive for. Lucas was enough motivation to make me into the warrior I needed to be.

I licked my lips and stared into his eyes. “Tomorrow you can kiss me all you want.”

Lucas smiled and cocked his head. “Promise?”

“Promise.” I walked out of the holding area with my stomach down by my feet.

I wasn’t sure I’d be able to keep my word, but I was going to fight like hell to get back to Lucas. I just didn’t know if it would be in one piece or not.

Chapter 15

MRS. WILTON BROUGHT EACH of us out a chicken sandwich and mumbled something about praying for all of us. It was appropriate that the town pray. We were going to need all the help we could get, and if God landed on our side, we might actually survive.

Remy stared at the ground as he slowly ate. As if sensing my gaze, he glanced up at me with bright green eyes that mirrored my own. Remy's hard features softened for a moment, and he took his last bite. He stood and crossed the distance.

"We never got to finish the conversation this morning." Remy took the seat next to me and remained quiet for a few minutes as he scanned the town green and the remaining three guards.

The five of us were the best shots in the unit. The rest of the Guard was stationed inside the church in case we failed. Except for Travis. He was told to secure the jail and make sure Lucas didn't get out.

"The fact you are my granddaughter doesn't change how things in the Guard work. I'm still your superior. You still have to follow orders," he said and leveled a hard stare at me.

I nodded. "I wish I had one of Gram's cookies," I said softly, changing the subject. I didn't want to be berated by Remy right now. I needed to focus on the things closest to my heart.

He let out a chuckle. "Me too."

"Did you love her?" I blurted. I didn't know why it mattered, but it did.

Remy studied the ground and then looked away. "Yes. But it wasn't enough. I didn't want to stay here locked in this town. I wanted adventure, and your grandmother was happy here." He shook his head and shuffled a foot in the dirt. "I left without saying goodbye. I was foolish enough to think that she'd wait for me, even though every single man in the area would have given away everything they owned just to be with that woman. She was a lot like you."

"Oh," I mumbled, not knowing what to do with the compliment.

"It took me a little over a year to figure out everything I cared about was back in Dakota. I went to see her bearing gifts, hoping she would forgive me." He sighed. "She was already married and had a son." He stood. "I never forgave her for moving on." He glanced at me. "And I'm angry that she never told me I had a family." Remy stuffed his hands into his pockets and rocked on his heels. "I'm not sure I would have allowed you to join the Guard had I known, even though you are the best shot I have ever seen in all my travels. That would have been a damn shame, too."

"If you were so angry, why did you honor her wishes?" I asked before I lost my nerve.

He smiled a sad smile. "I did that for you. Doc Wilton gave me the letter, and after I read it, I destroyed every possible thing within reach in my cabin. But I came to terms with the truth. And despite being a hard ass with you in particular, I've come to care about what happens to you, and it wasn't because you are my most skilled archer. It was deeper than that." He glanced out at the woods. "That was the hardest truth to face. I thought you were going to be executed today. I wanted you to have a little peace before you met your maker."

A lump formed in my throat, and I looked at the sky before he saw the tears gathering in my eyes. "We might want to get to our posts."

Remy followed my gaze and nodded. His hand landed on my shoulder, and he gave it a squeeze. "Shoot true."

I nodded and we held each other's gazes for a longer beat. He gave my shoulder one last squeeze and crossed to the pile of arrows and quivers. He split the sixty silver-tipped arrows evenly and handed each of us our quivers. Then he split the remaining arrows, which wouldn't kill the beasts, but it might slow them down so we could use our silver-coated knives. He passed out smaller weapons to each of us.

"I am good," I said when he went to hand a small stash of silver daggers to me. "I have a sword that the blacksmith gave me."

"At least take a couple and stash them in your boots. You are as accurate at throwing as you are with your arrow," he growled at me.

I took them, but did not stash them in my boots. Instead, I took my arrows and knives and lined them up in the dirt in a semicircle around me with the silver-tipped ones closest and the wooden arrows on the outside. I placed the strap to the sword holder over my head and adjusted it so the blade lay horizontally from my shoulder to my hip where it wouldn't interfere with my bow and arrow. I reached over with my right hand to make sure I could pull it free easily when the time came.

I glanced back at the church as the townspeople gathered with their casseroles and their plates like it was a town picnic instead of a vigil to see if we survived the night or not. I shook my head in disgust and caught Remy's same expression I was sure mine held as he looked on. I turned to the woods, focusing on the growing shadows. The sound of those gathered in the church silenced as the doors closed, capturing everyone within the steepled building.

Silence. I closed my eyes and focused on centering all my energy into one thing. The kill. The thrill of the hunt took over my form, rippling a chill from the tips of my fingers all the way to my core. I opened my eyes and focused on the fading light. Shadows elongated and the darkness behind them shifted. I couldn't tell what was shadow and what wasn't.

Twilight was upon us. My heart roared into overdrive as I threaded my first arrow. I knelt on one knee and held the bow steady, waiting for something to fix on. I had a clear view from between the posts and blocked the path into the center of the town.

I slowed my breathing, straining to hear movement, straining to see anything but shadows, willing my body and mind to embrace the calm surety that I would stop whatever came out of those woods.

With my arrow trained, I blinked at the shadows, daring the vermin to come into the fading light. As if I willed it, a shimmering glow filled the space. Rows of them, like an army formation as opposed to a solid line. My heart thundered, blasting through any sort of calm I had attained.

“Oh, Jesus,” I whispered and pushed the fear clawing at my skin away. I lined up my first shot.

Before the beast stepped onto the grassy knoll, it dropped dead from an arrow between its eyes. I threaded my next arrow and let another missile fly. It hit, like every other silver-plated arrow, until I found no more in my arsenal.

I had a handful of knives, but they wouldn’t hit the mark at this distance, so I strung up a wooden arrow. One after the other, they flew until I had nothing but the silver knives and the sword. A dozen wolves lay howling in pain alongside another dozen dead wolves. As soon as the arrows were gone, I grabbed the knives and stood.

It was as if they knew I was out of ammunition. With a loud snarl, they launched. I waited until I knew they were in range, and then the first four wolves went down with knives embedded between their eyes. I missed one, and the last one nearly took me down, but I parried and buried the knife in his neck.

With one sweeping twirl, I drew the sword and landed blows that normally would have been mortal wounds, but these beasts were fast and I only pissed them off more. They surrounded me, wary of the blade in my hands. None of them tried to bite me, which I thought was strange. If even one got a hold of me with their mouth, they could easily tear a limb off.

A long drawn-out howl came from the jail. My already pounding heart leaped into my throat. I couldn't take my eyes off my enemy to give Lucas any type of signal.

I swallowed and blew out a stream of air to get my focus. I moved into the ready stance that Remy had taught me, ignoring the snarling coming from the jail across the green. I stared down the rows of wolves surrounding me. I caught movement to my right and spun low to the ground.

The blade whistled through the air, slicing right through the beast's mouth, removing the top part of his head in one clean cut. The sword vibrated in my hands, but it had sheared right through muscle and bone as easily as cutting through warm butter.

The spray of blood doused my left side, the warmth sliding over me, taking the chill from my bones and replacing it with an icy revulsion.

The pack hesitated, eyes widening at the death of one of their own by my hand and not by an arrow. Their wariness amplified my confidence.

I repositioned myself. I think I may have smiled, because the pack snarled as one unified unit. They circled and I stayed in place at the ready.

“Who’s next?” I said, my voice a low, menacing growl that I hardly recognized.

I could have sworn I saw fear in a couple of the wolves facing me. When their gaze jumped to my right, I shoved the blade backwards, putting my palm on the end to hold it steady when I felt resistance.

Just as quickly, I drew it back. The thump behind me told me I hit the mark. I brought the blade back to the ready. Two down, too many to go. I took a breath, taking a second to open my ears to the battles in the distance. Panicked screams filtered in, but I couldn’t acknowledge them.

Not with another dozen wolves surrounding me. I caught movement in the back near the woods. I chanced a look, and the massive black wolf that appeared filled me with dread. His eyes narrowed at me, and he licked his chops.

I forced myself to pay attention to the beasts surrounding me. Had they moved closer while I was distracted? I swallowed the fear and reset my focus.

"Only two of you have the balls to try to take me down?" I said with a laugh, goading them.

It worked. Four rushed me and I spun, keeping my cool as blood spurted over me. Pain laced my hip as one of the wolves dug their claws into me before my blade took him out. I ducked and raised the blade. In one swipe, I disemboweled the bastard, blood and guts splattering all around me. I stood and shook myself. My hair clung to my cheeks in wet slaps. Then I spun, swinging the sword again. My arms burned from exertion.

A roar filled the air and caught me off guard. I spun toward the jail. The walls crashed down, and the beautiful gray wolf that had saved my grandmother came barreling out of the debris. Lucas wasn't the calm, docile wolf I'd first met. His bared teeth and horrific growl indicated a predator of such power and wrath that I nearly collapsed from the shock.

A growl behind me put me back into fight mode and I turned, swinging the blade, decapitating a wolf that had gotten too close. Before I could reset myself, paws hit my back with such force that I flew onto my stomach. The sword knocked from my grip, sliding out of reach.

I expected the sharp teeth in the back of my neck, but the wolf stood over me, growling. I rolled onto my back to face my last wolf and stared up at the underside of Lucas's head instead. His body blocked me from any of the other surrounding wolves. His growl sent tendrils of fear through me, but his protective stance warmed my heart. A mix of emotions ripped through me, leaving my entire form trembling. I rolled back on my stomach and scanned the ground for my sword.

The black wolf crept forward. His ears were back, and his muzzle wrinkled from his ferocious growl. His eyes held a murderous stare. The blade was closer to the black mass than to Lucas.

The rest of the pack widened their circle, letting the lead wolf into the center. Lucas lowered, the soft fur of his stomach tickling my exposed skin, but the blanket he provided didn't last. He launched at the black wolf.

"No!" I cried and scrambled for the blade. I climbed to my feet with the sword in my grip. My heart slammed the walls of my chest so hard, I thought it would rip right through my skin.

Lucas and the black wolf rolled away into the shadows, their growls and yelps filling the night.

The eight remaining wolves surrounded me with their teeth bared.

I could no longer hear the screams of the other guardsmen. My body numbed at the thought that the wolves in those directions won. The circle attacked as one unit this time. I think I screamed, but all I remember is fur and blood and the whistle of the blade.

An arrow whizzed by my face. I heard the wet sound behind me. In the direction of town, Remy had his last arrow drawn. Another wolf went down, leaving five to contend with while Lucas and the black wolf continued to battle in the darkness.

He dropped his bow, still running at full speed towards the massacre. Drawing his broadsword, he took the same battle form as I had been using. Two of the wolves that had been surrounding me peeled off to attack Remy.

My swings slowed to the point I missed one of the wolves. I glanced down and caught the reflection of a knife. In a twirl meant to maim, I swung the sword and dipped low enough to scrape the knife off the ground.

Remy cried out. My heart lurched. I spun in his direction and froze. Blood spurted from where his arm should have been. The beast who tore it off dropped the appendage and launches at Remy.

The knife sailed from my grip. It embedded in the wolf's eye before it could finish my grandfather off.

A yelp cut off behind me and I turned, forgetting about the three wolves still surrounding me. When the black wolf stepped out of the shadows with blood dripping from his teeth, I almost fell to my knees.

My ragged breath caught in my throat when the black beast transitioned into a man. He looked over my shoulder at the other wolves.

"Burn it down," he said with a gravelly voice that scared the living daylights out of me.

I spun, and two of the wolves had changed back into human form. They nodded and turned towards the church. A flash of silver flew through the air and buried to the hilt right through the spine of one of the men. He collapsed, dead before he hit the ground.

Only one person besides me had that kind of accuracy or strength in throwing knives. I turned to Remy. His gaze met mine, and then the only werewolf left in wolf form attacked him, tearing his throat out before I could get to him.

I swung the blade, but the wolf jumped out of the way. I went to swing around again, but a strong hand caught my wrist and bent it back. I cried out. The sword tumbled from my grip. The leader of the werewolf pack wrapped his hand around my throat and carried me to the post, slamming me into it.

Stars filled my vision. The grip on my throat loosened. I blinked my eyes until the blurring stopped and I stared into the cold hard eyes of the alpha wolf. He flipped me around and pressed me into the post so my head was turned towards the town.

"Watch them burn," he whispered in my ear.

"No!" I screamed and struggled.

His grip on me was too strong for me to do anything but smash my bones against the hard wooden pole. He grabbed a handful of my hair and put his nose to my neck taking a long, slow inhale.

"I have been waiting to take you down ever since you rode away from me on that black stallion."

I screamed my frustration, despite the pain my thrashing caused. The anger ignited in the center of my being and spun outward until my entire body felt like it had been dropped in a kiln.

He kept a grip on my hair and forced me into the road facing the church. The other wolf had slid a piece of wood between the door handles.

I twisted in the alpha's grip.

His hand snaked around my throat again, and he slammed me against his hard chest. I kicked at his shins. His hardness pressed into the small of my back and he just chuckled.

The chuckle nearly seized my muscles, sending a different fear through me. I wasn't afraid of dying, but that laugh chilled me into tremors.

He inhaled and sighed. "I love the smell of fear on the air."

The other wolf tossed a lit torch onto the front steps of the church where it rolled against the large wooden doors. Doors that were locked from the inside, but also barricaded from the outside.

"No! Please, please don't do this!" I struggled again, raking my nails down the length of his arms.

A sharp claw drew from the collar of my shirt down my shoulder, splitting both the fabric and the skin underneath. I screamed. Everyone I loved was lost to these beasts, and I was next.

The other two werewolves stepped in front of me, tearing my clothing while the leader's hand slid under the fabric of my ripped shirt, squeezing my breast, digging his fingers into my skin. I slammed my elbow into his stomach and kicked out at the other men, still fighting to get loose. To survive.

The alpha laughed in my ear.

"Your people will burn while they watch their red-headed savior become my bitch."

I shivered in his grip, aware that most of my clothing lay in tatters around us. His mouth covered my shoulder. It took a second for the pain to register as his teeth tore into my skin.

My scream tore at my throat, nearly bursting my vocal cords. The poison churned, working its way into my bloodstream. My scream wasn't the only one filling the air. I swore I would kill this beast if it was the last thing I did.

His hand moved from my breast down my body as I writhed from both his intent as well as the poison searing my veins. His other hand released my throat to explore. I slammed the back of my head into his face.

He stumbled back a step, just enough for me to twist from his grip. I turned in time to see a bloody blur launch at him. Teeth nearly tore the alpha's head clean off. I pivoted back to the other two werewolves, the men who killed Remy and set the church on fire.

Behind me, Lucas's visceral growls and the snap of bone echoed in my ears. The other two were staring with open mouths at the carnage behind me.

A high-pitched whistle caught my attention, and a silver-coated ax pierced the side of the closest wolf-man. The other one snapped out of whatever trance he was in and snarled at me as he transformed.

I spun towards where the blacksmith's sword lay in the dirt and sprinted. The wolf landed on me and I fell, scrunching my shoulders so he couldn't get a grip on my throat. That didn't stop him from raking my back with his claws.

Lucas attacked and they rolled off me. I sat up and turned towards the owner of the ax, relieved to see Travis pulling the weapon out of the dead man's head. I pointed towards the church and he nodded, holding up the ax as he ran towards the rising flames.

Travis slammed the ax against the wooden plank, shattering through it in one swing. He stumbled back and raised his plastered arm before using the blade to push the doors open. He had seconds to jump out of the way of the frantic townspeople as they flooded the street. It wasn't until they were far enough from the flames before the massacre around them registered.

"Wolf!" someone screamed.

I turned in time to see Lucas's wobbly step as he made his way to me, collapsing next to me. His massive tongue swept over the bite on my shoulder several times while his pained gaze met mine.

"It's Lucas," I said with a hoarse voice and put my arm around him to protect him from the frantic mob.

Travis maneuvered around in front of us, separating us from the townspeople. "Go home and lock your doors," he said, still holding the ax on his shoulder. His back remained facing us until the townspeople dispersed.

The adrenaline faded, and shakes gripped me. My teeth chattered, and my skin felt like I was on fire. My insides twisted, and I curled into a ball, unable to voice my pain. Bright lights bloomed in front of my eyes. My lungs seized. Lucas's whine sounded so far away.

Blinding agony gripped me, ripping through every muscle in my frame. I welcomed the blackness when it claimed me.

Chapter 16

SOMETHING HEAVY DRAPED ACROSS my waist. My pillow felt more like pebbles and dirt than the soft down I was used to. My brain remained foggy even as I cracked an eye. An old wool blanket covered me.

My eyes flew wide. I jerked into a sitting position on the town green. The shirt that had been draped over me slid and I gasped, pulling the shirt and blanket up to cover my bare chest.

A deep ache in my shoulder and back registered and I groaned.

My gaze fell to the man who had saved my life. Lucas looked up at me from the ground. His gaze fell to my shoulder, and he covered his face with his hands, rolling onto his back.

"I wasn't fast enough," he muttered.

I looked beyond Lucas at the green, and my hand flew to my mouth at the devastation. Dead wolves lay scattered, and the church was in blackened ruins.

"Tell me they got out," I said to Lucas.

He nodded and my chest squeezed. Tears sprouted and I cried. I didn't know why I was crying, but it seemed like the relief was too much to hold inside. I slid the shirt on and glanced at the cut short sleeve and the long sleeve.

"Travis?"

"Yes. He thought you might appreciate something to cover you up besides my bloody fur. He brought the blanket, too." Lucas stretched and winced.

His torso was patched with black and blue, and I reached out, running my fingers over the bruises.

"I'll heal," he said and stood.

Lucas didn't have a stitch of clothing on, and I blinked at his finely chiseled body. The thoughts parading through my head were totally inappropriate in a death field, so I turned away and situated the oversized shirt before handing him the blanket.

I climbed to my feet and took an unsteady step. Everything hurt. I winced and attempted to pass it off as just sleep-induced stiffness by waving him off when he went to give me a hand. But when I took a step and my knees buckled, I couldn't pretend I was okay.

Lucas caught me, and his groan clued me in as to his equally injured condition. The town started to stir, and I glanced at Lucas, at his bare skin.

"You need clothes."

He took the blanket and searched the ground until he found a knife. He sliced a hole in the center of the blanket and stuck his head through. As odd as he looked, it was better than walking around naked so anyone could see his fine form.

My gaze turned to the dead. My heart squeezed as I stumbled towards Remy. I dropped to my knees by his head, unfazed by the puddle of tacky blood surrounding him. I fluttered my hand to what was left of his face. One lone eye stared at the sky. The sorrow squeezing my chest let loose.

A howl came from deep in my throat. It was haunting and full of anguish, and I let it fully form as I sang my goodbye to my grandfather. I shivered when the sound died. Tears blurred my eyes, and I covered my face.

I had become what I abhorred.

"Come on, I think we need to get out of here while we can," Lucas said and helped me to my feet.

We limped away from the core of Dakota and into the woods leading to my grandmother's house.

Lucas pumped water into the bathroom basin and set it on the warmer.

"Get in," he said and pointed at the tub.

I blinked at him and then looked down at my bare arm. I was covered in dried blood. My hand shook as I reached for the edge of the tub. I stepped into the cast iron and looked up at him. I wasn't the only one streaked with blood and gore.

"I can't clean you while you are wearing a shirt," he said.

Normally, a request like that would have gotten the man decked in the jaw with all the fury my fist could carry, but this was not a normal situation. I stared at him as he lit the fire under the warming pot, debating on whether I should follow his request or not. I glanced down at my bare legs and shivered.

"I think we're going to need a lot more than just a pot or two." My voice shook.

Lucas smiled, but it looked more like a grimace. That was when I noticed his hands weren't steady. At all.

"Are you okay?" I asked.

A high-pitched laugh escaped from him as he stood with his back to me. "I wasn't fast enough," he whispered. His voice sounded haunted with his perceived failure.

"Lucas?"

He turned, his jaw tight and his lips pressed together. His eyes sparkled with unshed tears. I pushed myself to a standing position, but he shook his head. I wasn't sure if it was to rid himself of the tears or if it was to tell me to sit back down. When he didn't speak, I reached my hand out.

He stared at my dirty fingers.

I almost pulled my hand back, but Lucas finally took it in his. I drew him to where I stood and wrapped my arms around his neck, hugging him with all my might. Silence settled like a comfortable blanket wrapping around both of us. The hug lingered until he finally moved out of my grip.

"Soap?" he asked, his voice hoarse but at least his hands weren't shaking any more.

I pointed to the cupboard above the heating basin.

"Please sit," he said in a soft but firm manner.

I sank into the tub. He worked the bands holding my braid out and then poured the water over me. I gasped at the coolness. Lucas cranked the water pump, filling the basin again, and then he knelt next to the tub, cupping a handful of water. He drizzled it on my hair.

I stared at the red-stained water rolling off my skin and clenched my teeth against the unwanted shiver. Lucas grabbed a washcloth off the shelf and dipped it in the water before lathering it with the soap. His gaze met mine, and then he focused on wherever the cloth wiped. The gentleness in which he cleaned me magnified the horrors of the last few days, and tears escaped from the corners of my eyes in a silent deluge, mixing with the soap.

Lucas handed me the cloth. "Stand up."

I followed directions, and he pulled the stopper in the base of the tub. The water filtered into an empty pot beneath. After the last of the water drained, he placed the plug back in.

"Sit," he said, and as soon as I sat, another bucket of water doused me. This time, the tinge in the liquid was pink and not the vile red from the prior washing.

I ran the cloth over my body while Lucas pumped more water into the warming basin. He rinsed my hair and worked the soap in from my scalp to the tips of my red locks. His fingers worked in gentle circles, cleansing every inch of my head.

Instead of using the pink-tinted water to rinse the soap from my hair, Lucas opted to drain the water and start all over again. He continued the process until my tears dried up and the water ran clear.

All remnants of the battle washed away, but deep scars remained both on my back and in my heart.

He stood and extended a clean towel to me, and I climbed out of the tub, wrapping the soft cloth around my body. Just the feel of the fabric brought some normalcy back into my mind.

Lucas's hand cupped my cheek as he studied my face. "Go get some rest while I clean up, and then we'll figure out what we are going to do."

I nodded and turned before he stripped off the fashioned poncho. Another basin of dirty water went out the window, and I had a moment to wonder if I should reciprocate his kindness.

I paused at the door, and Lucas gave me a warm smile.

"It's okay. You need some rest," he said.

I couldn't argue with him. My body felt like it had been through a meat grinder. My eyelids drooped from the emotional drain.

In my bedroom, I glanced around the neat space and sighed, crossing to the dresser to retrieve undergarments and my night shirt. Just as I sat down on the edge of the bed, a knock at the front door interrupted my stupor.

The knocking persisted, so I shuffled to the door, cracking it. Travis stood on the other side with Doc Wilton. His eyes widened, and he recoiled with an open mouth.

His reaction shot heat to my cheeks, and I reached up, thinking I must be horribly disfigured, which would also explain Lucas's strange behavior.

"Your face is fine," Doc Wilton said and slid by Travis with his medical bag in hand.

"Then what is wrong with him?" I waved at Travis still staring at me like I had grown a second head.

"Nothing," Doc Wilton muttered, and his gaze dropped to the floor.

"What is it?" I insisted.

Travis fidgeted and stepped inside, closing the door behind him.

"Your eyes..."

"What about them?"

"They're green."

"They've always been green."

He laughed and glanced at the doctor.

Doc Wilton cleared his throat and set his bag on the table. "She clearly was the one who scared the town this morning," he said to Travis and then turned to me. "I'm here to examine you. Travis said you sustained some nasty wounds last night?"

"She's fine," Lucas said from the hallway.

I turned and any chance of concentrating on what either Travis or the doctor was saying ended. I stared at Lucas's towel-clad form. His wrists still carried the blackened burns from the silver. His bare torso had black welts from the silver knives that the Guard used to torture him before they dragged him to the posts. But even with all the scars, he was one fine man to look at.

A fire started in my toes and swirled through my body to the top of my head like a cyclone ripping over the plains. Hunger ached, and I blinked at the visceral reaction gripping me. His lips twitched, and he pressed them together suppressing a knowing smile.

"I've never seen eyes like that," Travis was muttering.

Lucas pulled his gaze away from mine. "Ruby is fine. The cuts on her back have already started to heal."

"Eyes like what?" I asked as Travis's words started to sink in.

"They are glowing green, not blue like his." Travis pointed to Lucas.

I raised my eyebrows. I had seen my fair share of werewolves, and every last one of them carried the same unique trait. Radiant blue eyes. I glanced at Lucas. He shrugged.

"Why don't you take a look at him instead." I nodded towards Lucas. "He's still got burns from the silver shackles you put him in."

Doc Wilton glanced at Lucas. "I don't have medicine that will help that."

I knew what would help. I turned, trudging down the hall to the back door where all the things Lucas and I had been carrying when the Guard arrested us still sat neatly piled on the steps. On top of my grandmother's blanket sat the aloe plant. I opened the door, and the stench hit me. I stumbled back a step and covered my nose.

"Smells like death, doesn't it?" Lucas said from down the hall.

I held my breath, opening the door to grab the aloe plant as quickly as possible. I slammed the door on the offensive smell, letting out a cough and a shiver.

He wasn't kidding. Now I knew why neither my grandmother nor I ever got attacked by werewolves. I wouldn't come within a hundred miles of that stench if I didn't have to. I crossed to him and handed him the plant.

"I'm fine," I said, echoing what Lucas had said earlier. "I just need some rest," I added and yawned.

Travis shifted his weight. A tangy scent filled my nostrils, and it was coming from him. I tilted my head.

“You’re... nervous?”

Travis chuckled and scratched the inside of his cast. “Well, um...” He glanced at the doctor.

Doc Wilton picked up his bag. “I wish you the best, Ruby,” he said and stepped out of the cottage, leaving us with Travis.

Travis let out a high-pitched laugh and stared at the floor. When he swallowed hard, I knew it was more than just nerves I was smelling.

“I’m not going to attack you,” I said.

He met my gaze. “You sure?”

“You’re my best friend. Why would I hurt you?”

“Um... because you were bitten by a werewolf last night.” He shoved his good hand into his pocket.

I shrugged, holding my hands out palms up in an effort to show him his logic was ridiculous. “I’m still me. I haven’t gone all crazy... yet. But if you don’t spill what’s on your mind, that may change.”

"Doc was sent with me to examine you to confirm your condition." He stared at the floor.

"Okay..." I rolled my hand in a circle prompting him to continue.

"They want you to leave." His gaze snapped up to mine, and he chewed on his lip.

It took a few moments of silence along with his steady gaze for what he was saying to sink in.

"After everything that I've done?" I waved in the direction of town. "Do you know how many werewolves I killed last night?"

"Yes. I do. And that is the only reason the Guard isn't here taking care of this mess," he snapped and then closed his eyes. His good hand curled in a fist of frustration. "I told them you insisted that I go open the church instead of help you. And that was *after* you were bitten. You still fought for them, and I wouldn't allow them to take your life." His gaze pierced mine.

I bit my lip. This was my home. I didn't want to leave. I glanced at Lucas for help, but he was no longer standing in the hallway.

"Where am I supposed to go?" I asked Travis.

"Your wolf-boy has a pretty nice place," Travis said and glanced around. "Where did he go?"

"To find something to wear," I said. The sounds of drawers opening and closing in my bedroom reached my ears. I wasn't sure Lucas would find anything at all that would fit him.

"I don't like this, Red, but it was the only way I could ensure they wouldn't put the two of you in front of a firing line. Remy isn't around to fight for you, either. At least a few of the townspeople took my side this time. Otherwise..." He pressed his lips together. When I opened my mouth, he put his hand up, palm facing me. "I already argued that your grandmother's house was far enough away from the town."

It was uncanny how he knew what I was going to say. I sighed and dropped onto the bench by the fireplace.

He crossed and took the space next to me. He took my hand, and we sat in silence, staring at our point of contact. Travis finally sighed and pulled his hand away.

"I have loved you since that first day your grandmother marched you out on the green and insisted Remy train you."

"Did you know Remy was my grandfather?" I said, trying to move this conversation in a different direction. I wasn't in the mood for one of Travis's undying love speeches.

He leaned away from me with his eyebrows arched. "Is that what you were howling over this morning?"

I nodded. "As much as I bitched about him, I did have a soft spot for him, even before we were told the news. He challenged me. Pushed me to be better. If it wasn't for him, I would be dead a dozen times over."

"I'm sorry," he said and slung his arm over my shoulder.

I winced and he pulled it back quickly, his eyes widening at my reaction.

"I'm healing. Not healed."

"Oh." He picked at his cast. "You really never felt the same about me, did you?"

There it was. The point-blank question I had dreaded for the past couple of years. I looked down at my hands. "You've always been my closest friend, and I love you for that. But that's where it ends for me. There's never been..." I trailed off because I didn't want to bruise his ego.

"A spark." His shoulders slumped.

I nodded and kept my gaze averted.

"But there is one with him, isn't there?" he asked with a low voice filled with bitterness.

I turned to him, a flare of anger on the surface. "Is that what you think? That Lucas is the reason for my not wanting to be romantically involved with you?" I stood and stepped away, distancing myself before the growl in my voice became something more.

He opened his mouth to answer, but his lips closed on whatever was lurking in his head.

"It wasn't Lucas. It was the fact I am not attracted to you that way."

He tried to hide the wince, but I caught it. He stood, his eyes hard, and he stepped close, looking down at me with those fawn-colored eyes. He moved fast, grabbing the back of my head and crushing his lips to mine.

I blinked at the pressure on my lips, and my heart jolted in surprise, but there was nothing else behind the physical contact. Travis slowly pulled away, his eyes wide like he had just had the world's biggest epiphany. He let out a giggle and covered his mouth as his cheeks flushed red. It was the oddest reaction to kissing me, and it turned my insides into a defensive mode.

"No spark." His eyes searched mine, but it wasn't that begging look that I had seen for years.

If I had known a kiss would have stopped him from pining for me, I would have allowed it the first time he attempted it. He ran his hand through his hair and laughed.

"Why are you laughing?" I asked, a little put off by his reaction.

"Because he just realized he has been chasing a fantasy all these years," Lucas said from the hall.

We both spun towards his voice. Lucas leaned against the wall with his arms crossed. The tension in his shoulders and arms wasn't lost on me. He had seen the interaction, and I was sure he heard every word. Tan dungarees hung on his hips that he must have found in the back of my grandmother's closet, and they looked like they were painted on. The length fell short of his ankles, but at least he found something.

Travis gave me a shrug.

"And we have to leave Dakota," I said.

"So I heard. Is Ruby allowed to pack up, or are you going to run her out of town like she's a common criminal?" he asked.

I caught the warning in his eyes even though his tone was conversational.

"She can take whatever she wants," Travis said. "Midnight is out front, along with your bow and the sword you had last night."

“The sword belongs to the blacksmith.”

“He’s the one that insisted you take it. He was one of the people that stood by me, along with Doc Wilton and a few others.”

I didn’t know what to say. That weapon was gorgeous. I wondered if I would need it now that I had tainted blood pumping through my veins.

“How much time do I have to pack?”

“You need to be out of Dakota by dark.”

A lump formed in my throat, and I swallowed it. I didn’t want to succumb to the wild pendulum of emotions mixing in my blood. I nodded and started towards my room but stopped before going down the hallway.

“Can you do me a favor?” I asked Travis.

He nodded.

“Do you think you could saddle up the mare in the corral for us and bring her around front for me?”

“Sure.” He turned to leave. “Do you mind if I visit you some time?” he asked with his back to me.

“I’d like that,” I said. Travis left via the front door, and I turned to Lucas. “You’re right. The corral smells like death.”

Chapter 17

I STEPPED OUT FRONT to load my saddle bags on Midnight, and my horse whinnied, stomping his hoofs. His eyes went wild just like they had when Lucas approached him in the stable the other day. I grabbed the reins to keep him from rearing.

"It's me, Middy," I said and placed my hand on his jaw.

He whinnied again, but stilled at my touch, searching my eyes. Then he nudged me like he was afraid of me.

"It's okay. I know I smell different. So do you," I whispered and ran my hand down his neck. My stomach growled, and I licked my lips, trying to staunch the growing hunger in my belly.

I turned as Lucas came out with another set of saddle bags and my grandmother's folded quilt. His mare was tied up next to Midnight, courtesy of Travis.

"You good?" Travis asked from the doorway.

"Almost," I said and handed the saddle bag to Lucas. "I want to do a last walk-through."

"Take your time," he said in a soft voice that assured me we had all the time in the world.

But I knew the clock was ticking. My hunger was starting to bite into my focus, and I didn't know what would happen when I gave in to the craving for something hot and bloody.

Travis stepped to the side as I crossed the threshold of my grandmother's house for the last time. I pulled the key off the wall and held it in my palm. The weight of it didn't match that of the sorrow at the pit of my stomach. I crossed to my room. There wasn't anything in the bedroom that I had any emotional attachment to, but when I stepped into my grandmother's bedroom, her warm scent filled my soul.

I hadn't gone in here to pillage her things. But now that I stood in her bedroom surrounded by the warmth of her, I wanted to pack everything into a box and keep it with me at all times. I crossed to her bureau and ran my finger along the fine wood grain.

I pressed the back of my hand to my lips. I caught my reflection in the mirror on her desk and reached for it, mesmerized by the glowing green eyes looking back. The minute my hand touched the handle, I yelped. Fiery pain singed my fingertips, and I stared at the mirror with wide eyes. The handle was silver.

I turned on my heels and nearly ran out of the room, but paused at her bed and grabbed the pillow. This held her scent, and I prayed it would hold it through a long ride through the valley to Lucas's place. I needed my grandmother with me, or otherwise I might give in to the growing need accosting me.

I gave Travis a quick hug and slid the cabin key into his hand. "The house is yours if you want it," I said and turned to Midnight, mounting him with one quick step into the stirrup.

"Red?" Travis said as Lucas coaxed his mare next to Midnight.

I met his gaze and gave him a pained smile. There was nothing more to say, so I nodded and tapped my heels on Midnight, moving him forward.

"Take care," Travis called as the woods swallowed us up.

Lucas took the lead and when he gave a hee-ya, his gray mare became a lightning bolt. I tightened my grip on the reins and kicked Midnight, and he took off at a full gallop until he caught up to the mare.

Lucas glanced back at me with a teasing grin. It was the most playful look I had seen on him since we met. My heart burst into a wild rhythm as we passed the Dakota line into the badlands where no one had traveled until the night my grandmother fell down into the ravine.

The woods on the other side of the plains were as thick and lush as they had been the other day, but this time, there wasn't a threat in the area, so I had a chance to appreciate the scent of pine and brush of the leaves as they passed over my exposed arms.

I pushed Midnight forward until Lucas and I were side by side. His smile was infections, and his eyes sparkled. I just wanted to hop onto his horse and hold him tightly against me. Actually, I wanted to stop the horses and ride him instead.

Heat filled my cheeks at the thought. While there was never chemistry with Travis, the opposite could be said about Lucas. Even his glance set me alight with the dirtiest of thoughts.

We breached the woods moments later, riding across the expanse of saw grass towards his cottage and the farm beyond. The thought of beef and chickens set off the saliva glands in my mouth and the growl in my stomach.

Lucas slowed his horse, and I followed until we were outside his home. He piled our stock onto the porch and set the aloe plant on a wooden table in the shade before he took Midnight's reins from my hands.

"I'll let you figure out where all that needs to go while I get these two set. I'll cook us up something to eat when I get inside, okay?"

My stomach made a glorious noise.

Lucas smiled. "I'll hurry," he said and led the horses away.

I tested the door. It opened freely, and I took his advice, carting the saddle bags packed with my clothing inside. On my last trip, I grabbed the aloe plant. Now that my adrenaline had faded, the burn on my hand raised its ugly head. I sat amidst my pile of everything I owned and cracked a spine off the plant, squeezing the ooze onto my hand. I gently worked it into the black welt across my palm.

It stung at first, but then the soothing coolness seeped in and I closed my eyes. Lucas shuffled in the house but didn't say a thing. I kept my eyes closed, focusing on the acuteness of my hearing and smell. Lucas reminded me of a fresh breeze mixed with a sexy musk. I just wanted to lick every inch of him.

The closer he got, the more my heart thundered in my chest, and when his lips captured mine, my eyes flew open at the instant fire that engulfed me. He was on his hands and knees in front of me, his gaze intense.

He licked his lips, and I nearly moaned. How could a man have this much command over my body?

"You said I could kiss you all I want today."

A soft groan escaped from my lips. The slow smile that formed dimples in his cheeks made me forget about the pains in my stomach. Hunger gripped another part of my body, but I wasn't ready for this intensity. I scrambled to my feet. When I took a step back, I tripped on one of the saddle bags.

Lucas was fast. He caught me in his strong arms before my head had a chance to connect with the wall. He spun me so I faced the wooden logs and pressed against my back. His warmth engulfed me. His fingers tickled my neck as he moved my hair away so his tongue could trace the line of my throat. A low growl of contentment flowed from him as he nibbled my earlobe.

His hands traveled from my sides to the buttons of my shirt, nimbly releasing each one until it hung on my frame. His fingers scraped my skin as he peeled the fabric off my shoulders. The pressure on my body released, and my shirt drifted to the ground. I looked over my shoulder, and his eyes were locked on my back. He gently traced my scars, his touch creating a tingling in my skin.

The slide of his hands from my back around my sides to my breasts created a shiver. My arms broke out in gooseflesh as his mouth found the back of my neck again. He rolled my nipples between his fingers until they were hard nubs before his hands traveled down the length of my stomach in a soft caress.

He fumbled with the buttons on my pants as he sucked and nipped at my neck and ear. With a growl of frustration, he gave up on trying to be civilized and yanked each side of my pants, sending buttons pinging into the wall. My hands pressed against the wall, pushing my body into his, feeling his excitement against the small of my back. When his hand dipped inside my undergarments and traced the sensitive bud between my legs, I moaned.

“This is going to hurt,” he whispered.

My heart stopped at his words, and then his teeth severed my skin in the same place that the alpha bit me.

I bucked in his arms, pushing him away and turning.

“What the hell do you think you’re doing?” I snapped.

All the heat that had been pooling in my belly evaporated. Anger replaced it, along with the sensation of whatever poison he possessed filtering in through the bite.

“Replacing the alpha’s mark,” he said and wiped my blood off his chin.

I crossed my arms over my exposed chest and glared at him. “Why?”

“So every wolf we encounter knows you’re mine.”

“I’m nobody’s bitch,” I said and reached down, swiping my shirt off the floor. I slipped it on and growled at his audacity.

His intense questioning stare pierced through my anger. A crease appeared between his eyes, and his head cocked.

“That is what that bastard called me. His bitch. If you think this means you own me, you are sorely mistaken." I waved at the bloody welts on my shoulder and went to step away.

Lucas stepped close, blocking my retreat. He threaded his hands into my hair on either side of my face and crushed my lips under his. I opened my mouth to protest. The sweet tang of blood followed his tongue and I nearly dropped to my knees. Time stilled and an icy heat spun from the wound in my shoulder. His saliva mixed with my blood, creating a whole new fascination for the man kissing me.

I gasped as he broke the kiss, wanting more, but still aggravated with him for the possessive mark. I broke away from his strong grip and grabbed his shoulder. Before I knew what I was doing, my teeth sank through his skin. He tasted delicious, and I forced myself to step away when his wince registered.

"Why did you do that?" he asked, grabbing his bleeding shoulder.

"Because if you can be all possessive, so can I." I propped my hands on my waist and stared at him. I licked the remnants of blood still left on my lips, and my stomach cramped again. "I'm hungry."

Lucas's eyes blazed, and he turned towards the kitchen, stomping across the house like I just broke his favorite toy. The slamming of pots and pans announced his aggravation.

I turned my attention to the mess I made of his living room. It took me a couple trips to move all the bags into one of the two bedrooms in his cottage and then I stepped back into the kitchen. A plate of scrambled eggs sat on the table along with a fork. He slammed his plate down opposite mine and dug into his food without a word.

I had no idea what I did to deserve this treatment, but my stomach decided that it needed attention before Lucas. I scooped up a forkful of eggs, and they were just as good as they had been the other morning. When I took my last bite, he ripped my empty plate from under me. Anger oozed from him while he cleaned the dishes.

When he finished, he leaned against the sink with his head bowed. It was time to address this head on.

He turned when I stood from the table, and I crossed the distance and put my hands on his chest. His heart pounded against my palms. I took a moment to tune in to my senses. His musky scent remained the same, thrilling me with each inhalation.

"What's wrong?"

Lucas laughed and glanced at the ceiling before he met my gaze. "You're the alpha," he whispered.

I cocked an eyebrow. "What?"

"In this little pack..." He pointed between the two of us. "You are the alpha."

"Just because the alpha..."

"That's not how it works. If the alpha of that pack had survived..." Lucas snorted a laugh and maneuvered around me, putting a little distance between us. "If he had lived, he would have had to challenge you or obey you. The only time you would have been his bitch would have been that evening before you fully absorbed the venom."

I narrowed my eyes at him. I didn't understand.

"Do you hear my commands in your head?"

"No." I laughed, thinking he must be insane.

"If I was your alpha, you would."

I stared at him. *Come here*, I demanded in my head, testing out his theory.

Lucas pressed his lips together tightly and stepped forward.

"Whoa. Wait a minute..." I put my hands up, trying to ignore that nagging sense of power. I didn't know how this was even possible. I didn't want this.

"No. You bit me. You put your claim on me. Now I'm subject to whatever you command of me."

"This is what you expected when you bit me?" My voice rose to a high pitch. The thought of being at anyone's beck and call turned my stomach.

He closed his eyes and hung his head. His cheeks flared red. "Yes."

The fact he admitted it blanketed me in a cold sweat. "How do I undo it?"

This time he crossed to stand in front of me. "There is no undoing it. At least your heart is pure, not like that shit who bit you. I guess things could be worse. I could be his bitch." Dimples appeared in his cheeks.

I pressed my lips together at his lame attempt at humor. "Why am I alpha?"

He shrugged. "Spirit of the warrior. You have it. I don't."

He reached out and tucked my hair behind my ear. His touch ignited the heat inside me, and I suppressed the urge to wish his arms around me. I needed to know if what was here between us was real, or if I was in the same fantasy world as Travis had been.

"Lucas, why did you kiss me in the jail cell?"

He cupped my cheek. "Because you stole my heart. You are everything I am not. Brave. Fierce. Beautiful." His thumb traced my cheekbone. "And I just wanted to taste you before I died." He leaned forward and pressed his lips to mine again. "Why did you kiss me back?" he whispered against my mouth and pulled back, waiting for me to answer.

Just being in this close proximity increased my heart rate. "I couldn't help myself, especially since there was something in the air between us. I couldn't tell if you felt it or not."

"The spark?" he asked, and dimples appeared in his cheeks as a smile danced on his lips. "Yes. It hit me like a lightning bolt the moment you rounded that rock in the ravine."

Heat flushed my cheeks and I smiled. "I didn't feel it until I was standing in this room with my arrow trained on your back, and you turned to greet me." I tilted my head. "You knew I was there, didn't you?"

"I knew the minute the bedroom door opened. You smelled like sweet honey and a summer's day and all I wanted to do was devour every inch of you." He smiled. "I still want to devour you."

"And this has nothing to do with *my* desires?"

He pulled me against him. "No."

His mouth was on mine, and every inch of my body ached for him. Our tongues tangled in an intense kiss that yanked the air from my lungs. When he pulled away from my lips, I whined.

"But it will have to wait until morning," he said and glanced at the window.

The setting sun painted the room in a red blaze that matched the fire burning inside me. I didn't want to wait.

He looked back at me. "*I* want to take my time, so you, my sweet alpha girl, will just have to have a little patience."

A pout formed on my lips, but a nagging itch tingled along my spine. I blinked at the sensation and flexed my shoulder blades together to staunch it.

"Clothes," he said with urgency as the light faded. He nearly ripped my shirt off, and I thought maybe my influence actually jump-started him into action. It wasn't until he stepped away that I understood.

He yanked his shirt over his head and kicked his boots off, stripping his pants a second before he fell to his knees. I stepped back, watching in fascination.

A yelp yanked from my mouth, and the itch in my spine turned into a torrent of rippling agony. I dropped to my knees the moment Lucas became a full-fledged wolf. Tearing fabric combined with popping joints, and I gasped as I looked down at my hands. They were covered in red, grey, and white fur spread over massive paws that matched Lucas's. My transition was much faster than his had been, but not quite the easy shift that the werewolf pack exhibited last night.

I wondered if I could transition at will or if I was at the mercy of the night, like Lucas. I swept my tongue over my teeth, dragging my attention away from my thoughts. The sharpness of my fangs held marvel, as did the sweep of my tail. The power of my new form pulsed in my veins.

Lucas closed the distance in two strides, and ran a wet tongue over the side of my face. I rubbed my nose to his and stepped closer, wrapping my head over his back in a canine hug.

I wanted to run, to play, to hunt. I wanted to learn my speed, my strength, my agility, and Lucas seemed to understand. He crossed to the front door and paused, glancing back at me.

His musings in the jail flooded to the forefront of my mind, and I trotted next to him, sensing his unease. I licked his face to ease his fears. My stomach rumbled in concert with his. The transformation used every last bit of energy the eggs he had cooked provided. I needed more food.

Doubt shaded his blue eyes.

He didn't realize the rules of the Dakota Guard still reigned true in this foreign body. Even though the urge to hunt overwhelmed me, *what* I hunted still mattered.

Humans were not on that list. Neither were the livestock in the fields behind us, even though they did smell divine.

The hesitation in Lucas evaporated, and his tension eased. With his paws, he unlatched the front door, and it opened on the night. I stepped out onto the porch and scanned the woods before I glanced at Lucas.

Try to keep up, I thought and then exploded from my haunches. I flew through the air, landing on my front paws before my hind legs hit the ground and pushed off. I ran so fast, the wind pulled tears from my eyes and my lungs burned. Lucas matched my pace, and his tongue lolled out the side of his mouth as he panted.

I slowed and came to a stop on a small grassy knoll, stretching my limbs. Lucas nipped my haunches, and I whirled on him, jumping up and putting my teeth on the back of his neck. He rolled under me, and before I knew it, I lay on my back under him as he stared down at me with his big wolf smile.

I climbed to my feet and froze with my nose in the air. Venison filled my senses. A deer was downwind, and I turned in that direction. Lucas turned with me. My mouth watered at the thought of the deer, but without a bow and arrow, I had no sense on how to take it down with wolf teeth.

I glanced at Lucas. *Teach me.*

He led the way with steps so light that even I had to strain to hear him. The doe came into view, and Lucas nodded his muzzle to the right. Crouching, he moved to the left. I followed his lead, veering to the right of the deer. Her ears straightened, and her head rose just as we came even with her front shoulders.

Lucas launched and his mouth clamped down on the underside of the deer's neck. I followed, but I landed on the top of the deer, clamping down on the back of its neck. I jumped off, twisting the deer's head enough to snap its spine.

Warm blood flowed into my mouth and I swallowed, cherishing the sweet taste. We tore at the carcass, both eating greedily until our bellies were full and only bone and sinew were left.

We licked each other clean before Lucas led me back to the cottage. He led me to a soft mat in the corner of the porch that I hadn't noticed before. When he curled around me, I let out a soft sigh of contentment. I breathed in the night, thankful to be alive and at Lucas's side. My future revolved around the werewolf next to me, and I knew it would be filled with unending adventure.

A pair of white doves landed on the railing near us and fluttered their wings. I stared at the birds, so out of place in the northern pacific woods. I blinked my eyes to make sure I wasn't seeing things, but the birds remained in place. The doves almost glowed in the darkness.

I shifted, cocking my head at their intense stares. In concert with each other, their wings spread, and they took flight. On the breeze created by their wings, I could have sworn I heard my grandmother whisper how proud she was of me.

The End

Continue the Fractured Fairy Tales collection with Cinder.

About J.E. Taylor

J.E. Taylor is a USA Today bestselling author, a publisher, an editor, a manuscript formatter, a mother, a wife, a business analyst, and a Supernatural fangirl, not necessarily in that order. She first sat down to seriously write in February of 2007 after her daughter asked:

“Mom, if you could do anything, what would you do?”

From that moment on, she hasn’t looked back.

In addition to being co-owner of Novel Concept Publishing, Ms. Taylor also moonlights as a Senior Editor of Allegory E-zine, an online venue for Science Fiction, Fantasy and Horror, and co-host of the popular YouTube talk show Spilling Ink.

She lives in New Hampshire with her husband and during the summer months enjoys her weekends on the shore in southern Maine.

Visit her at www.jetaylor75.com to check out her other titles.

If you enjoyed RED, you will love the rest of

J.E. Taylor's Fractured Fairy Tales!

FRACTURED FAIRY TALES

RED
CINDER
BRAVE
TANGLED
FROZEN
SNOW
SPINDLE
JASMINE
BELLE
HOOK

OTHER TITLES BY J.E. TAYLOR you may enjoy:

YOUNG BLOOD

Duty and fate collide when a cocky young alpha finds his forbidden mate.

Robby Young never anticipated meeting his true soul mate on the first day at the Monster Defense Academy, especially considering relationships with other members of the agency are strictly prohibited.

When that girl ends up listed as his partner, Robby has to muzzle his wolf to keep her safe.

If he falls prey to his desires and crosses the line his father set, he'll sentence his partner to a position in front of the firing squad.

WICKED HEART

Waking up to blood smeared walls certainly does not instill calm. Quite the opposite, considering I had locked my house up tight with deadbolts, sigils, and safety spells to ward away evil.

And I went to bed alone.

With no memory of a struggle and no signs of a dead body, there's only one logical conclusion. One of the demons we hunt at The Monster Defense Agency broke into my home.

My insatiable cravings clue me into exactly what I'm dealing with, and now I need to track the bastard down and fillet his ass.

Otherwise, my life will be forfeited, and I will become the hunted.

CROOKED SOUL

Escaping from captivity brings its own special challenges. Like dealing with PTSD, along with major trust issues.

When an ancient vampire arrives from overseas, she comes with baggage from a past long before I was born. And she is hell-bent on revenge.

Not only are we trying to dodge the monsters, but we are back on the radar of the Monster Defense Agency, and they are pissed.

If Robby and I can't get our shit together, either the MDA or the master of the vampire who nearly destroyed us will finish the job.

TAINTED MIND

No one in the agency is safe from our wrath.

I am the last of my kind, deemed a monster by the Monster Defense Agency. But the MDA does not understand the hell their duplicity has unleashed.

Robby and I are now on our own hunting expedition.

Our target: the head of the MDA.

Although, it isn't just one man pulling the strings. It's a highly complex network that is more like a damn hydra. When you extinguish one, another pops out of the woodwork.

Two against an ancient organization that trains monster-killers and that knows all our tricks is even harder than it sounds. It's going to take all our skill and intelligence to kill this beast.

And being caught is not an option.

Monsters, trust issues, betrayal, and a near death experience.

What else could go wrong?

The end of life as we knew it didn't come with a nuclear blast. It didn't come with the deadly impact of a hurdling asteroid. No. It came in a wave of illness that swept the world with fear, and in our quarantined silence, the monsters awoke.

Leviathans, serpent kings, and dragons came forth from the bowels of the Earth. The season of the dragon began with fire and fury and ended with a new world order. One in which these giant terrorists held all the power.

When Mikhail St. Clare betrays the monsters by saving me from death at their claws, I cannot trust the last remaining dragon shifter. Not when humankinds' survival is at stake, and he had a hand in our near extinction.

The only thing we seem to agree on is our desire to annihilate the leviathans and unseat the Serpent King. Our personal futures depend on ridding the earth of these murderous overlords.

We thought crossing the leviathan-patrolled city where every corner hides a hideous death was our most lethal hurdle. But building a bomb large enough to wipe out an entire species carries its own insane levels of danger.

One wrong move and we could destroy everyone living in New York instead.

Find these titles and more at

www.JETaylor75.com!

Made in the USA
Middletown, DE
10 July 2022

68518328R00139